D0323826

THUNDERCLUCK!

WRITTEN BY
PAUL TILLERY IV

CO-ILLUSTRATED BY
PAUL TILLERY IV AND MEG WITTWER

ROARING BROOK PRESS
NEW YORK

For Sadie
(And for anyone else who might be a "World's Best Big Sister")
—P.T.

For my family, who've stayed strong by my side
through all my shenanigans
—M.W.

Text copyright © 2018 by Paul Allen Tillery IV
Illustrations copyright © 2018 by Paul Allen Tillery IV and Meg Wittwer
Published by Roaring Brook Press
Roaring Brook Press is a division of Holtzbrinck Publishing Holdings Limited Partnership
175 Fifth Avenue, New York, NY 10010
mackids.com

Library of Congress Control Number: 2018936552
ISBN: 978-1-250-15528-3

Our books may be purchased in bulk for promotional, educational, or business use. Please
contact your local bookseller or the Macmillan Corporate and Premium Sales Department at
(800) 221-7945 ext. 5442 or by e-mail at MacmillanSpecialMarkets@macmillan.com.

First edition, 2018
Book design by Christina Dacanay
Printed in the United States of America by LSC Communications, Harrisonburg, Virginia

1 3 5 7 9 10 8 6 4 2

PROLOGUE

In ages past, in distant realms, in tales of myth and rune,
In worlds beyond the one we know, beyond the stars and moon,
When evil had a dinner plan, and hope was at its end,
A hero found his courage in the quest to save his friends.

The story of this hero is a little odd, you see,
For neither mortal man of Earth nor mighty god was he.
And now, at last, the time has come to recollect once more
The legendary Thundercluck: the chicken . . . of Thor.

TIME TO BE BRAVE, THE CHICKEN thought.

The volcano towered above. Thundercluck stood on the bridge to Castle Igneous. The chef awaited inside. The bridge was hot, but the chicken shivered.

"Buk-buk-bagock," he said.

Time to be brave, he thought again. *My best friend is counting on me.*

Buk-buk-bagock, he thought. *Buk-buk-bagock, indeed.*

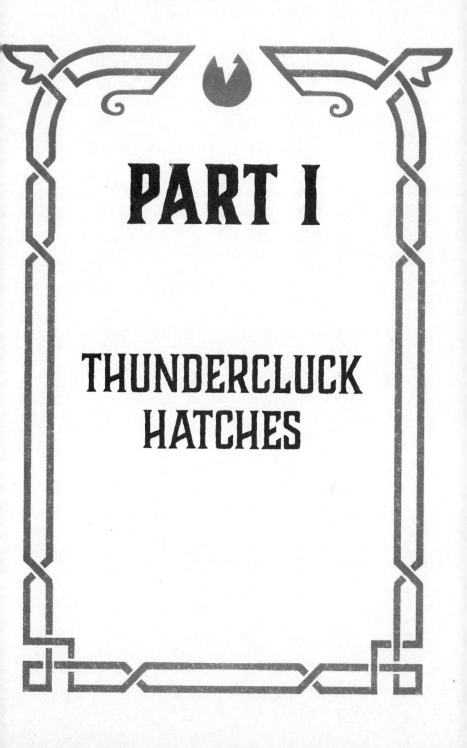

PART I

THUNDERCLUCK HATCHES

CHAPTER 1
THE POWER HATCH

TWELVE YEARS AGO . . .

CLANG!

The magic hammer met the frying pan, and sparks erupted in the night.

"For the last time," bellowed Thor, swinging his hammer with each word, "you"—CLANG!—"cannot"—CLANG!—"cook"—CLANG!—"Hennda!"—CLANNGGG!

Gorman Bones staggered back, blocking the hammer with his pan. He straightened his chef's hat and apron, and through his mustache he growled, "I'll have that chicken yet! It could be the greatest meal this realm has ever seen!"

"Never!" Thor shouted. He hammered again, driving the chef away from Asgard's chicken coop. "I've told you already, you crooked cook—I forbid you to broil my bird!"

Hennda, Thor's darling hen, sat on the coop's roof. She cocked her head. Gorman stared at her with ravenous eyes, then glared at Thor.

"You're always telling me what I can't do!" he barked. He pitched his voice to mock Thor's. "'No stealing from the garden, Gorman.' 'No open flames near the

cat, Gorman.' 'No cooking people's pets, Gorman.' Well, I've had it! I'm going to eat that chicken!"

Thor narrowed his gaze, his red beard lowering as he frowned. He held his hammer to the sky, and storm clouds covered the stars. "Then so be it, chef. Your fire magic is no longer welcome here. The only thing you'll dine upon"—the hammer began to glow—"is THUNDER!"

At Thor's command, a lightning bolt flashed from the clouds above. In that same moment, the chef swung his pan down, shooting flames at Thor's feet. The Thunder God jumped and stumbled, dropping his hammer to the ground. With a booming crack, the lightning bolt split in two.

One branch of the lightning struck the chef, who vanished in a puff of smoke. The other struck Hennda, who jolted into the air with a squawk.

"BWAAAAHK!"

The bird landed with a thud, eyes wide and feathers

smoking. She was shocked and singed, but otherwise unharmed.

"The bolt's power was divided," Thor said to himself. "Thank fortune Hennda's jolt was not enough to fry her." He looked where Gorman had disappeared. "Was the rest enough to slay the cook?"

Hennda blinked, then gave a little wiggle, and with a cluck, she began to lay a glowing egg.

"Bwak," said Hennda. The egg landed beneath her, casting a pale blue light.

Thor climbed onto the coop and held his fingers to

Hennda's cheek. Sitting on the egg, she cooed and twitched her tail feathers.

The thunder had woken more Asgardians and drawn them to the scene. At the front of the crowd was Brunhilde, an infant girl with wings. In other worlds, she might have been called an angel or a cherub. Here in Asgard, she was called a Valkyrie.

Brunhilde yawned, rubbed her eyes, and squinted.

Under Hennda's rump, the egg glowed brighter. Beams of light shone through her feathers. A high-pitched hum filled the air, and the egg began to wobble. It quivered at first, then shook so much the whole coop rattled. Hennda remained seated, wide-eyed, shaking, and determined to keep the egg covered.

For a moment, all went dark, and then a thunderous crack sent Hennda flying through the air. The egg had hatched, and in its shell sat a baby chick wearing a horned helmet. His feathers cast a golden glow. He gave a little chirp, and a tiny lightning bolt shot from his beak.

Hennda fluttered back to the coop and stared at the

baby bird with Thor. All the Asgardians were still except Brunhilde, who trotted to the newborn chick. She patted his fluffy feathers, and he chirped with glee, emitting a burst of sparkles.

Brunhilde giggled. She poked his beak, thought, and said, "Thunder . . . cluck."

Later that night, the Castle of Asgard was peaceful once more. Brunhilde rested her head on her pillow, and Thundercluck snuggled beside her. Hennda

snoozed by the bed. Thor stood on the balcony, wiping the soot from his hammer.

The god smelled smoke, but he saw no fire. A chef's hat drifted before him, and a voice whispered, "You haven't seen the last of me..."

And the hat vanished in the wind.

CHAPTER 2
THE PROMISE

FOR THE NEXT FEW YEARS, THUNDER-cluck and Brunhilde were inseparable. They played in Asgard's golden fields and swam in shimmering lakes. Thundercluck lived in the coop with his mother, and Brunhilde often slept on its roof, cuddling the baby bird.

In the Castle of Asgard, Thundercluck was allowed only in Brunhilde's room. Animals were not permitted in the halls, and certainly not on the Royal Couch. Now and then, though, Brunhilde would sneak him on the couch anyway. She tucked him inside a purse that had belonged to her mother, a rare memento of a family she had never known.

As a baby, Brunhilde had been adopted by the gods Odin and Frigg, king and queen of Asgard. No one ever spoke of Brunhilde's birth parents.

Thundercluck quickly became like a little brother to the girl. She would hug him tight and say, "You're my family now!"

As the years went by, Thor marveled at the young chicken's powers. Thor needed his hammer to summon lightning, but Thundercluck could generate it from within. *Someday,* thought Thor, *that chicken may be the strongest of us all.*

With greedy Gorman gone, Asgard's new chef was a

friendly god named Andhrímnir. Brunhilde had trouble saying that, so she called him Andy. Andy knew Thundercluck was a friend, not a food.

A time of peace had fallen upon Asgard, and all was well.

Thor watched one day as Brunhilde and Thundercluck climbed a tree. The playmates giggled and chirped, and the Thunder God smiled ... but then a shadow crossed his face. King Odin had appeared.

"My son," Odin said to Thor, "you must bring those two to the castle at once." Beneath his bushy gray brows, the elder god's face was grim. "We have all been summoned," he went on. "Saga has had a vision."

Deep in the Castle of Asgard, curtains hid the Seeing Throne. Dozens of Asgardians had gathered in the chamber before it and were waiting for Saga, Goddess of Vision and Foresight.

All was quiet at first, but soon the audience began to murmur. Bragi, the bard, plucked nervously on his harp. Thor made his way to the front of the crowd, holding young Brunhilde high. Little Thundercluck sat on her shoulder.

The curtains parted, and Saga stood from her throne. Everyone hushed but Bragi, who strummed a majestic tune. Saga spoke:

Well met, ye gods and goddesses; you're looking fine and brave.
Alas, I fear I've called you here with tidings ill and grave.
Some years ago when Gorman fell,
we thought that Thor had won,
But Gorman Bones endured, and now . . .
his threat has just begun.

Many in the crowd gasped, and a string on Bragi's harp broke with a sharp twang. All had thought

Gorman had perished, but Saga's visions were never false. When silence had fallen once more, the goddess continued.

I know the chef lives on, my friends,
and though it chills our hearts,
He's studying the darkest
of the culinary arts.
In some dark chamber,
some dark pantry,
some dark breakfast nook,
No longer is he just a chef—
he's now an Under-Cook.

The good chef Andy shivered. The idea of an Under-Cook—a chef who had been to the underworld and back—belonged only in scary stories and nightmares. The goddess went on.

I know not where, but now the Cook has built himself a kitchen,
And trust, he's not forgotten how he hungers for some chicken.

Although he's far away, I fear there's trouble yet to come;
The Cook no longer wants our hen . . .
next time he'll want her son.

Saga's words echoed through the hushed chamber. All eyes turned to Thundercluck, who broke the silence with a high-pitched "Buk-bwok?"

The gods then burst into an uproar; everyone liked Thundercluck, and no one liked that evil Cook. Brunhilde grabbed the bird from her shoulder and held him to her chest. Fury burned in her eyes.

Saga raised her hand, and the crowd went quiet once more. In a regal tone, the goddess concluded:

The Cook's return is now foretold, and this I know is clear:
Young Thundercluck's in danger if we choose to keep him here.
We have to send him far away, and hide him out of sight,
And there he'll have to stay until he's old enough to fight.

"No!" Brunhilde cried, holding Thundercluck tighter still. With a look of deep sadness, Saga met the child's gaze, but the goddess had spoken. She sat back down on her throne, and the curtains closed.

The crowd again grew noisy, and Thor turned to Brunhilde. "We must act quickly," he said. "We shall hide him today."

"There's . . . There's no other way?" Brunhilde's face softened, and the fury in her eyes gave way to tears. Thundercluck chirped in her arms.

"I fear not," Thor replied. "I must consult my father; Odin will know where the bird can hide. Take Thundercluck to the Bifrost. I will meet you there."

A rainbow shone on a platform of rock. This was the Bifrost; Brunhilde had heard it was a bridge to another realm. She stood at its base, looking at the symbols carved in the stone. They were runes, the mystic form of writing Asgardians used to harness magic.

Brunhilde held Thundercluck as they watched the sunset. They heard footsteps, and the little chicken chirped.

Odin and Thor approached. Thor held Hennda, who had a small suitcase under her wing. Odin bore his spear and an empty glass bottle.

Thor set Hennda on the ground. She waddled to Brunhilde and nuzzled the child's leg. "Hennda knows what must happen," Thor told the girl. "Soon Odin and I will take the birds to their new home."

Odin pointed his spear at the rainbow rising from the Bifrost. "This magic light will warp us to another realm," he said, "a world separate from our own. There we shall hide Hennda and Thundercluck among foreign chickens."

Thor patted Hennda's briefcase. "You'll be an odd bird there," he told her. "Don't you show off how well you can fly, and keep an eye on that son of yours."

"As for Thundercluck," Odin said, "we shall take his magic away, lest his thunderbolts reveal his hiding place." He handed the glass bottle to Brunhilde. "You must help us withdraw his powers."

The elder god tapped the tip of his spear on a rune, and a shimmering birdbath appeared on the Bifrost. "Brunhilde," he said, "put Thundercluck upon this birdbath, and take this bottle into your hands." Brunhilde pouted, but she followed the instructions. "Now, Thor," Odin continued, "present the sock."

Thor gave Brunhilde a sock made of Asgard's finest wool. "Brunhilde," Odin said, "take that holy sock, and use it to rub the chicken's feathers."

She cocked an eyebrow, then started brushing Thundercluck with the sock. Despite her worries, she smiled when his feathers began to stand on end. Soon he was a perfectly round ball of fluff, and arcs of lightning zapped from his helmet to the birdbath. Brunhilde stepped back to Hennda's side.

"Good, good," Odin said, "that's brought his charge to the surface. Now, Brunhilde! Open this bottle and hold it before the bird!" He gave the bottle to Brunhilde.

She popped its cork, and the Bifrost's runes began to glow.

Odin raised his spear in one hand, and with the other hand he drew a scroll from his pocket. "I bear an incantation from Saga," he said. He opened the scroll and read:

This bird has thunder magic; feel the sparkle and the shock.
We've called it to the surface now, by sacred woolly sock!
As king of Asgard I command, so let it not be doubted,
Into that bottle, I declare . . . a holy Power Outage!

With a flash of light and a crack of thunder, everything went dark. The Bifrost rainbow stopped shining, and even the sun seemed to vanish. Then a blue light glowed; it was the bottle, emitting the same pale hue that Thundercluck's egg had cast the night he was born. Brunhilde held the bottle in her hands, and its light shone through her fingers.

"And thus . . . his power is disconnected," Odin said. The jar continued to glow, and the rays of the

Bifrost and the setting sun became visible once more.

Thundercluck was unhurt, but nonetheless he quivered. Brunhilde set the bottle down. She traced her fingers through his feathers. "You're cold!" she whispered, and she pulled something from her pocket. "Here, have this. I wanted it to be for your birthday . . . but I guess now is better."

She held a tiny vest that matched Thundercluck's helmet. She slipped it on the bird, and his shivering stopped.

Thor came up beside them and crouched to look Brunhilde in the eye. "I'm sorry, dear, but the time has come." He stood and turned to the Bifrost's rainbow light. "Odin and I must take the birds to the realm of Midgard," he said. "That is where the

Vikings live, and they call their world ... Earth. There Thundercluck must stay until Saga says otherwise."

"Can I go with him? Or at least visit?" Brunhilde meant to look at Thor, but her eyes were fixed on Thundercluck.

Odin answered, "No, child, here you must stay. Your place is in Asgard."

Thor cleared his throat. "For the sake of secrecy, there is one more effect of this spell. Soon Thundercluck will sleep, and when he awakes, he will have lost all memories of our realm ... and of you."

Brunhilde felt like she had ice in her chest. She hugged the bird tightly. "Goodbye, Thundercluck. Even if you don't remember me, I won't forget you."

Thundercluck pressed his cheek against hers, and then Thor lifted him away. Odin scooped up Hennda, and the gods walked into the rainbow. They vanished in a flash of color and light, and Brunhilde was alone.

For a long time, Brunhilde stayed on the Bifrost. When the sun had set and the stars came out, Saga joined her. Brunhilde wiped her sleeve across her cheeks. "I'm not crying," she said.

Saga picked up the glowing bottle and a fallen golden feather. After a quiet moment, the goddess said:

> *I know that this is hard for you, and it's okay to cry.*
> *You learned today how much it hurts*
> *to say the word "goodbye."*
> *But lift your chin and set your gaze*
> *to look beyond the sorrow;*
> *We cannot change the past, my dear,*
> *but we can shape tomorrow.*

Brunhilde took a deep breath and stopped fighting her tears. They rolled down her cheeks, and she felt a new sense of calm.

She looked at Saga, then lifted her eyes to the stars.

Someone out there wants to hurt Thundercluck, Brunhilde thought. *One day,* she promised herself, *I'm going to be strong enough to look out for my friend.*

CHAPTER 3
SEPARATE WAYS

THE GODS AND THE CHICKENS ARRIVED
in Midgard, the realm some called Earth. Moonlight
shone in the sky.

Nearby stood a Nordic farmhouse with a chicken-
shaped weather vane on its roof. The weather vane
looked bored.

Thor knocked on the door, and an elderly couple answered. They were Olga and Sven, Midgard's finest
chicken farmers.

"Greetings," Odin said, and Hennda squawked from
her perch on his arm. "We come from Asgard with
urgent need."

"And with chickens," added Thor.

"By the gods," Sven whispered, "you're ... you're the gods!"

Olga said nothing. She looked at the chickens and gods with a curious smile.

"Allow me to explain," Thor said, and he told them of Thundercluck's peril.

"Are you certain they'll be safe here?" Olga asked. Beside her, Sven now held Hennda and Thundercluck. They warbled in his arms.

"The Under-Cook only hungers for Asgardian birds," Odin said, "as do monsters across the realms. As long as no magic draws an evil eye, these two shall live as birds of Earth. Danger shall not find them."

Thor patted Hennda's cheek and said, "Farewell, my feathered friend."

Hennda gave a knowing wink.

Thor turned to Thundercluck. "These Vikings,"

he said, "their world is the earth and the sea. Yours is the sky. May some part of you always remember that."

Odin and Thor went back to the moonlit hills. A rainbow shone upon them, and in a flash the gods were gone.

Thundercluck shuffled close to his mother, snuggled beneath her wing, and went to sleep.

Farm life was strange for Thundercluck. Olga and Sven treated him well, but the other birds thought he was weird.

For one, they puzzled over his vest and hat. As far as they were concerned, no self-respecting bird would wear such things. And they found his wandering even more bizarre, especially when he ventured away from the feeding bucket. He was always exploring the woods, climbing trees, and seeing how high

he could perch. He could flutter his wings to hop short distances, but he wished he could soar.

More than anything else, though, he wished he had a friend.

Sometimes at night, while all the chickens slept in their barn, Hennda would wake to see Thundercluck's spot empty. She would go outside and find him on the roof, gazing at the stars.

Back in Asgard, Brunhilde began her training as a Battle Maiden. Her wings grew strong enough to fly, and Thor gave her a shield and a crystal sword. She still carried the purse from her mother, but now she called it her Battle Bag. She trained daily in Valhalla, the hall of Asgardian heroes.

Soon she could harness magic in the shining crystal blade. She trained her wits as well, taking top honors in the Spelling Bee of Runes. In her spare time, she practiced knitting to relax.

With every step, with every test, with every bruise and cut, young Brunhilde thought to herself:

For glory!

For Asgard!

And most of all, for friendship—for Thundercluck!

After years of study, it was time for a trial of skill. Brunhilde entered Valhalla's training chamber.

Inside stood Odin, Thor, and a stage made of sacred stone. The stage held three marble statues: a pair of armored warriors and a single towering lion. A scroll rested in the lion's jaws.

"Welcome, Brunhilde," Odin said. "You have proved the might of your arms and wings. It is time we test your head as well."

Brunhilde nodded, and Odin went on, "The realms abound with monsters and giants, all of them bent on our destruction. Some want our riches. Some want our food. And some . . . are simply grumpy. Today you shall face such a beast."

Thor stepped forward. "A Valkyrie, Brunhilde, must have not only power, but also wit. She must find the warriors worthy of Valhalla, and she must lead them into battle." He raised a helmet with a visor and a pair of wings. "This helmet is a Valkyrie's sacred crest."

Brunhilde tried to look calm, but she found herself smiling.

"To complete this phase of your training," Odin declared, "one final step remains." He pointed to the scroll in the marble lion's mouth. "Pick up your diploma."

Brunhilde's smile dropped. *That's it?* she thought. *I worked my wings off all these years just to pick up a sheet of paper?*

Odin cleared his throat, and the sound echoed through the chamber.

Disgruntled, Brunhilde fluttered to the lion statue. With its head bowed and its eyes closed, it almost looked gentle. *Well, this is . . . not exactly satisfying,* she thought. She reached for the scroll, and the lion's eyes sprang open.

The marble creature leapt away, and the two statue warriors burst into motion. Both held battle-axes. Both swung at Brunhilde.

BONNG! CLANNG! In a flash, Brunhilde had her weapons drawn, blocking one axe with her shield and the other with her sword. The warrior girl pushed with her arms and twirled, driving both axes away, and the statues stumbled backward.

Brunhilde focused on her sword, and its crystal blade began to glow. She twirled again and swung an arc of

light, hitting both of her foes. They shattered into pebbles and dust.

Brunhilde gazed around the chamber, seeing candles, pillars, and tapestries, but no lion. On the far wall, a banner dangled almost to the floor. Just below its fringe, Brunhilde saw a tail.

She smiled and charged at the banner, but the lion was quick! It pounced from behind the banner and climbed a wall, then hung by its claws from the rafters. The diploma dangled from its mouth. With a flap of her wings, Brunhilde flew to the scroll, but the lion darted away. It dropped to the floor and dashed beneath a table.

No matter how she chased it, Brunhilde could not catch that cat. They clattered around the chamber, blowing out candles and knocking over furniture. Soon, the girl was pooped. She stood panting on the stage. Across the room, the lion sat. It scratched its ear with its foot.

All right, Brunhilde thought, *if I can't come to you . . . I'll let you come to me.* She strapped her sword and shield to her back, and she opened her Battle Bag. The lion pretended not to care, but out of the corner of its eye, it watched.

Among the bag's contents was a ball of yarn for knitting. With a little hum, Brunhilde sat on the stage and tossed the ball from hand to hand. The lion was transfixed.

Under the creature's gaze, she let the yarn drop to the floor. She smiled at the cat and said, "Oops."

The lion charged her way, bounding at full speed. It leapt for the yarn with its mouth wide open. The scroll came loose, and Brunhilde darted aside, reaching for it.

WHOOSH!

The lion had the yarn...and Brunhilde had her diploma.

"Good show!" Odin shouted. "Good show, indeed." He clapped his hands, and the lion froze. It was once more just a statue, now with a ball of yarn gripped between its teeth.

"Stand proud, Valkyrie," Thor said, placing the helmet

on Brunhilde's head, "and open the scroll. It bears tidings from Saga."

Brunhilde raised her eyebrows. Saga was distant, reclusive, and not one for small talk. *I wonder if it just says, "Sorry for hiding your chicken,"* Brunhilde thought. She unrolled the parchment and read:

You've earned the title, Battle Maiden, mighty as can be,
So raise your wings, and let them sing: Brunhilde, Valkyrie!
Your name will soar across the realms; we all agree it's true.
I'm proud of what you've grown to be, and I believe in you.

A locket fell from the scroll and into Brunhilde's hand. She opened it to find something Saga had plucked from the Bifrost years ago: a golden feather from Thundercluck.

On the farm, Thundercluck had grown bigger, but no less restless. He had no training, no studies, no knitting to keep him busy.

One day he looked especially lonely, so Sven and Olga invited him into their house. They went to a room with a rug on the floor.

"We have something to show you," Olga said.

Thundercluck looked around. He saw nothing unusual.

Sven winked and said, "Just one second."

Olga moved the rug to reveal a flat door hidden below it. She opened the door, and a staircase descended into darkness.

"Buk . . . ba bok?" Thundercluck said.

Sven grabbed a lantern from a shelf, and Olga smiled at Thundercluck.

"Come with us," she said. "It's a secret."

CHAPTER 4
THE COSMIC TREE

THE STAIRCASE LED TO A SHADOWY
basement. It smelled like woods and mystery. Thundercluck squinted, but he saw nothing.

Olga dipped a stick into the lantern's fire and used it to light several candles. As the candles burned brighter, Thundercluck noticed a tapestry on the wall.

"This is the cosmic tree," Olga said, pointing to the image on the tapestry. "It's called Yggdrasil."

EGG-dra-sill, Thundercluck thought. *I like that!*

"Yggdrasil contains all of existence," Olga went on. "Let us tell you how it came to be."

In the beginning, there was nothing . . . nothing but the Ginnunga Gap, a wide expanse of emptiness. No people. No places. No worlds. At one end of the gap there was heat, and at the other there was cold.

The heat and the cold were far apart, but after eons of drifting, they met. When hot met cold, they formed a cloud of mist. It twisted, and thundered, and swirled, and from this cloud came the first beings in existence.

One being was Ymir, the first of the giants. Ymir was powerful, and he held the potential to make new realms and new life. But more life would mean more sharing, and Ymir wanted to keep his power to himself.

Another being was Odin, the first of the gods. Odin was wise, and he wished for the universe to grow.

Odin asked Ymir to help him create new worlds, but the giant said no. A battle broke out between them.

They clashed, and sparks flew high into the air. These became the stars in the sky. The struggle was legendary, and in the end, Odin defeated Ymir. The giant became crystal and moss, and a tree sprouted from his body.

This was Yggdrasil, the cosmic tree of life.

Thundercluck stared at the tapestry, barely aware his beak was open.

Sven saw the chicken's wonder. He grinned.

"Yggdrasil contains our world and more," Olga went on. "Every living thing has a place in the realms, which are held by the tree's branches."

Thundercluck blinked in confusion.

Olga pointed to the tree's branches on the tapestry. They held circles bearing views of other worlds.

"These orbs are the nine realms," she said. With a twinkle in her eye, she added, "There's more to the creation story—and there's more to existence than we can see."

The cosmic tree rose, and Odin found himself whisked to a new realm, a world upheld by the tree. Odin was joined by fellow gods, and together they discovered separate worlds: nine realms that could only be reached by magic.

Some are realms of fire, ice, and death. But others are realms of beauty and grace.

In the middle of the tree, we humans live in Midgard, the realm we call Earth. Above us, at the highest level of the tree, the gods live in the realm of Asgard. They rule a kingdom of magic and glory.

From Asgard they watch us, vigilant against danger. Odin the All-father reigns as king. His wife, Queen Frigg, holds the keys to all the kingdom, and she spins the clouds we see in the sky. Together, they have a son: Thor, God of Thunder.

Thor, Thundercluck thought, and he felt a tingle in his feathers. His eyes locked on the top realm's circle.

Sven grinned wider.

"Thor is the mightiest god!" he said. "Every time you hear a thunderbolt, that's Thor banging his hammer!"

The chicken found it hard to stand still. For so long

he had felt something was missing, and these stories almost made him feel whole.

"And guess what!" Sven added. "When warriors here on Earth are deemed worthy, they rise to Valhalla, the hall of Asgardian heroes. They're chosen by Battle Maidens, the Valkyries!"

The chicken felt a flutter in his chest. Olga put a hand on Sven's shoulder, and she gave him a look that said,

That's enough, dear. Sven ignored her, and he leaned close to the bird.

"And you know what, Thundercluck?" he whispered, "Asgard has chickens, too!"

Thundercluck's eyes and beak opened wider.

Olga cleared her throat pointedly, but Sven went on. "Oh, yes! And Asgardian chickens are smarter than the average bird. They understand when people talk, and legend has it . . . they can even read!"

Thundercluck looked at the tapestry and saw the word "Yggdrasil."

I . . . I can read.

Then he thought of the farm's other chickens, who had spent the afternoon chasing a worm by the feeding bucket.

Olga cleared her throat again and said, "Yes. Those are nice stories, dear. Odin, Thor, and the Valkyries fend off evil so the rest of us can live quiet lives down here. Now, Thundercluck, why don't you go outside and play?"

Thundercluck took one last look at the tapestry, then dashed up the stairs and outside, flapping his wings and running in circles all the way.

Olga turned to Sven with worried eyes. "I only wanted to show him the tree," she said. "We mustn't tell him too much!"

"Oh, relax," Sven answered. "He needed some company, and look how happy he is! We can't tell him everything . . . but we can let him dream."

In another realm, a bone-white hand reached for a shadowy bookshelf. The knuckles traced over ancient tomes, then clutched the one titled *The Recipe Book of the Dead*.

Skeletal fingers cracked open the book and flipped through its tattered pages. "Ahh yes, here we are," whispered a smoky voice. The book sat open to its darkest chapter: "How to Feed Your Demons."

Then the voice chuckled, and it rose to a cackle that echoed through the shadows.

CHAPTER 5
THE CHICKEN'S CALL

IN THE REALM OF ASGARD, BRUNHILDE was on patrol. After the helmet ceremony, her elders had started assigning her missions, but most of the "missions" were just delivering packages and walking laps around the kingdom. She called it the Busywork of the Gods.

She came across a tower, an Asgardian outpost at the kingdom's edge. She expected to see lanterns and sentries on its roof, but it was bare. One of its windows was lit, and two shadows moved within.

Brunhilde flapped her wings and flew to the window.

She heard voices inside and listened, hidden from view.

"Worrisome ... most worrisome indeed," Odin grumbled. "Our foes grow ever stronger."

"Yes," Thor replied, "but now we have Brunhilde, who may yet become the greatest Valkyrie of all."

"Perhaps," Odin said, with a distant look in his eye. "Top three, at least."

Brunhilde smiled and thought, *Well, that's a nice backhanded compliment.*

"But I fear," the elder god went on, "the monsters are rising in power too fast—"

They heard jingling keys, and then the door to the stairs flew open. There stood Queen Frigg.

"My queen," Odin said. "How did—"

"Saga said we would find you here," Frigg answered as she entered the room.

Odin raised his brows and asked, "We?"

Saga walked silently through the doorway.

"She came with me for a secret council," Frigg went on, "for she has had another vision."

Brunhilde clutched the locket that hung around her neck.

"Buk-bwaack!" Hennda called proudly as Thundercluck ran by. He had grown into a fine chicken. His helmet shimmered in the afternoon sun.

On a nearby hill, Sven and Olga tossed grain to the main flock. Thundercluck charged in their direction, and all the rest of the birds scattered in a frenzy.

"Bok-bok-bok-bok!" Thundercluck whooshed by, his clucks fading into the distance.

Sven and Olga stood amid a cloud of feathers. "There he goes again," said Sven, smiling as he tied the grain bag. "Always running around."

"Indeed," said Olga. "I wonder where he wants to go."

At the Asgardian tower, Saga cleared her throat. The other gods sat silently. Saga took a long look at the window where Brunhilde was hiding, then turned to the gods and spoke:

Despite the might of Valkyries, and Vikings under Thor,
Our kingdom faces danger like we've never known before.
A thousand monsters gather now, their aim to doom us all;
Without another hero's help . . . Valhalla soon will fall.

Thor stood. "We can fight them," he said, but Odin glared at him. Thor sat back down. Frigg nodded at Saga, who went on:

We sent a magic bird away, and now that bird has grown;
The chick is now a rooster, and it's time to bring him home.
When monsters come! When danger knocks!
When evil runs amok!
We need ourselves a chicken, now—
we need our Thundercluck!

Brunhilde's heart jumped.

Thor gripped his hammer, and in a low voice he asked, "But what of the Cook? If we bring the bird, will Gorman Bones not follow?"

The goddess answered,

Oh yes, the Cook is dangerous; that much is true, my friend.
No doubt he's out there smoldering, and plotting grim revenge.
But now our need is grave, indeed! Our kingdom is at stake,
So bringing back the chicken is a risk we have to take.

Outside, Brunhilde could no longer stay quiet. She leaned through the window and cried, "I will go!"

"Brunhilde!" Odin barked.

"You were spying?" Frigg demanded.

"How long have you—" Thor started to ask, but as he spun around, his chair broke. He fell to the floor with a crash.

Saga raised a finger to her lips, and all went silent. She gestured to Brunhilde as if to say, *Go on.*

"I will go to Midgard. I will bring back Thundercluck!"

Saga smiled, and from the sleeve of her robe she pulled a glowing jar. It was the vessel holding Thundercluck's powers, hidden all those years ago. It was lightning in a bottle.

Locking eyes with Brunhilde, the goddess commanded:

Then hold this bottle up against his feathered chest and see:
The bird will gain his thunder back, and learn his destiny.
A storm is rising in the night, and it's about to thicken;
The time has come at last to tell the truth about the chicken.

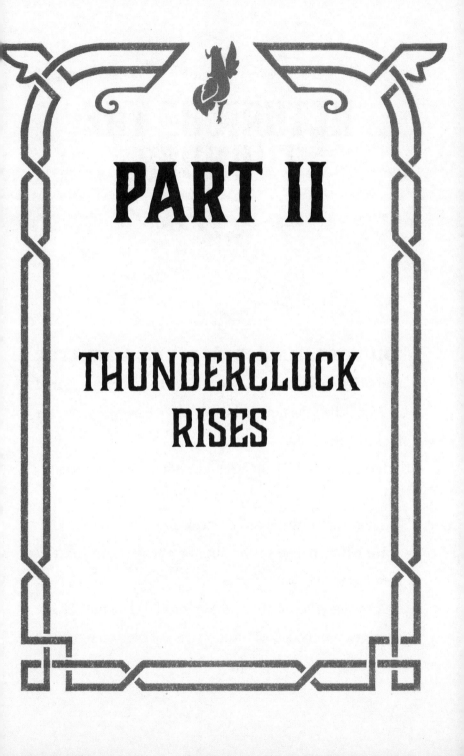

PART II

THUNDERCLUCK
RISES

CHAPTER 6

RETURN OF THE THUNDER

THUNDERCLUCK STOOD ON A HILLTOP and beheld the rising dawn. The other chickens stared at him. They darted their eyes elsewhere whenever he looked their way.

"Bwak, bwak," Thundercluck sighed. *Alas, just another day.*

Then the feathers on his neck stood up.

He felt a change in the air, and the grass in front of him flattened.

A rainbow beam shone down on the flat spot. Thundercluck jumped back, and with a flash of light the rainbow vanished. A girl with wings stood in its place, her eyes hidden beneath her helmet.

All the other chickens scattered, squawking frantically as they ran. Thundercluck stayed on the hill, transfixed.

"Thundercluck!" the girl sang, and she wrapped her arms around his neck. His brows went up, and he slowly raised a wing to return the hug. The girl lifted the helmet's visor, and her eyes twinkled. "It's been a long time," she said.

"Buk . . . bugak?" the chicken replied.

"Sorry," she said. "There's a lot you need to know." She held her sword to the sky and said, "I come from Asgard, realm of the gods!" Then she smiled and added, "And so do you, Thundercluck."

The chicken stared at her, then slowly began backing away.

"Have you ever wondered," she said, "where your helmet came from? Or why that vest always fits, no matter how big you've gotten?"

The chicken paused. He tapped his vest with a wing and thought, *It does fit nicely.*

"Your clothes have Asgardian magic, and so do you and I," the girl said. "I'm Brunhilde, a Valkyrie of Valhalla. And you're...well, the term Thor used was 'demi-god chicken,' I think."

Thundercluck blinked. He was skeptical, but excitement stirred within him.

"Anyway," Brunhilde said, "the important thing is, we need you. And you'll need this." She drew a glowing bottle from her bag, and the chicken felt a tingle in his wattles.

"Ten years ago we hid you here, and we hid this from you. This is your thunder. This is part of who you are." She looked upward. "Back in Asgard, monsters are coming to destroy our home ... and if you take your thunder back, you can help us fight them."

A million thoughts bounced in the chicken's head, but he knew two things: he liked this person, and he liked that bottle! There was something familiar about Brunhilde. He stepped forward, but she raised her hand.

"I have to warn you," she said. "If you take your powers back, you'll face your first test as a warrior. Do you know the Woods of the West?"

The bird paused. In all his wanderings, that was the one place Sven and Olga had forbidden him to go.

"Asgard has a fortune-teller," Brunhilde said, "a goddess named Saga. She says there's a demon wolf in those woods—and it's hungry."

The chicken gulped.

"Oh, you're safe right now," Brunhilde said. "Chickens without powers are too bland for a demon wolf. But if you take your thunder back, well ... let's just say the wolf will come for breakfast."

Thundercluck shifted his weight.

"The bottom line is, I know you're a dreamer," Brunhilde said. "I am, too. If you take this step, though, for better or worse . . . all those dreams are about to get real."

Brunhilde held the jar in one hand, and with the other she twirled her sword. "If you're ready for adventure," she said, "then I will aid you in battle. But the choice is yours."

Thundercluck stared at the glowing bottle. He had always yearned for excitement, but he had never thought about the fear that might come with it. His heart was thumping, and he wondered whether it was from joy or fright—or both.

He turned toward the barn, and to his surprise he saw Olga, Sven, and his mother watching. The Viking farmers smiled, and Hennda's eyes gleamed with pride.

"We knew this day would come!" called Olga.

"We believe in you!" called Sven.

"Buk-bwaak!" called Hennda.

Thundercluck turned to Brunhilde with resolve in

his eyes. He took a step forward, lifted his chin, and said, "Bagock!"

Brunhilde smiled and unplugged the cork.

The demon wolf awoke to the sound of thunder, and it rose to all fours with a yawn. Its nostrils sniffed the air . . . and it licked its lips.

Thundercluck felt like a million stars were shining inside him. Storm clouds rolled overhead, and he wanted to soar above them. After years of just fluttering, he felt like he could fly. He felt like if he stretched out his wings, he could touch the gods themselves.

Then he heard the growl.

"The wolf approaches," Brunhilde said, and her helmet's visor clinked down. "Sven! Olga! Take the other chickens into the barn. We'll handle this."

Thundercluck watched them scurry inside.

"The wolf only wants you, Thundercluck," Brunhilde

said, "but everyone else is safer out of the way. Here it comes!"

Over the hills, the wolf came prowling. First they saw its ears, and then its hulking body came into sight. Thundercluck's eyes widened. The beast was bigger than an average cow, and it looked meaner than a mad one. Its dark fur had highlights of blue, and its eyes glowed bright and menacing. It growled again, and the ground shook under Thundercluck's feet.

"Be careful, my friend," Brunhilde said. "Your power is thunder. Mine is light. The wolf's magic is sound, and it's loud."

Thundercluck nodded, and in his mind echoed two words: *my friend*.

"WOOF!"

The air rippled as a sound wave shot forth and flew at Thundercluck.

Brunhilde grabbed the chicken and pulled him sideways. The sound wave shot by and hit a rock, which burst into shards. The wolf growled, then . . .

"WOOF!"

It barked again at the bird.

"Behind me!" Brunhilde shouted. She whipped up her shield, which began to glow. The sound hit the shield with a BONNG, and the magic dispersed. It rattled the grass at her feet.

"My turn," Brunhilde said, and she swung her glowing sword. An arc of light shot out. Thundercluck poked his head from behind the shield to watch.

The beast growled again, this time in a lower pitch, and the air before it shimmered. Brunhilde's light hit the sound wall and burst into a shower of sparks. The light scattered in all directions, and the wolf stood unharmed.

"Hmm ... all right, then," said Brunhilde. "I'll draw its attention, and Thundercluck, you zap it!"

The bird turned his head completely sideways. *Zap it?*

"You'll remember how"— she patted his shoulder, and

beneath her visor she smiled—"hopefully very soon." With a WHOOSH, her wings spread wide as she darted to the left.

Thundercluck gawked as she flew. The wolf barked another wave of magic, but she dodged it—barely. The sound wave grazed her wing and continued across the sky. It hit Sven's weather vane, blasting it off the farm's roof.

Brunhilde landed on the ground with a roll. Her wing was sprained, but not broken.

Thundercluck's heart pounded. Brunhilde was the first person to ever call him "friend," and that wolf wanted to hurt her. The clouds rumbled overhead, and the chicken felt something powerful building within him.

He felt like a hammer was pounding in his chest. His feathers vibrated. Instinctively, he pointed his wings toward the wolf and gripped the ground with his chicken feet. The storm clouds went utterly silent.

"Bagock!"

KRA-KOOWWWWWW!

A bolt of lightning seared the air and struck the wolf on its side. The beast stumbled and dug its claws into the dirt.

Thundercluck's beak fell open. *Did I just do that?* Then he looked at the wolf's face. *Uh-oh.* Little strands of lightning still buzzed on its fur. It looked angry.

"WOOF!"

The beast gave its loudest bark yet, aiming right at Thundercluck. The chicken froze. He had no idea how to block an attack. His feet refused to move. And that sound wave was zooming his way . . .

BONNGG!

Brunhilde was back in front of him, her shield raised and glowing. "This is getting noisy, huh, buddy?" she said. "That was a good shot you took. Its hide must be tough . . . We'll have to find a soft spot!"

The chicken looked at the wolf, which snarled with rage. The beast took a breath so deep it sucked all the grass between them toward itself.

"WOOF-WOOF-WOOF-WOOF-WOOF!"

Thundercluck crouched as the sound waves came flooding at them. Brunhilde kept blocking the noise, and her boots dug into the dirt. Her shield still glowed, but it began to flicker.

"It's too loud!" she shouted. "I can't fly until my wing heals, and I can't focus on my magic! I wish! This dog! Would STOP BARKING!"

I panicked a moment ago, thought Thundercluck, *but I can't do that again . . . Have at ye, foul beast!* He cried "Buk-buk!" and leapt high into the air.

"Wait," called Brunhilde, "I can't keep you safe up there!"

In midair, the chicken closed his eyes and counted to the barking rhythm. He spread his wings wide, and he felt magic coursing through them. Then, in sync with a bark, he flapped his wings hard. A shock wave blasted outward from the flap.

The shock collided with the bark and repelled it back at the wolf, catching the beast in the chest. The wolf coughed and shook its head. It tried to bark again, but only a wheeze came out.

"Nice work!" said Brunhilde, lowering her shield and letting it darken. "Maybe now we'll have some peace and qui— Never mind."

The wolf charged at her, snarling and baring its fangs. Thundercluck landed between them, and he tried to summon another bolt, but the beast pounced too soon.

Brunhilde pushed Thundercluck aside and somersaulted under the wolf. She lifted her shield, and a dome of light flashed upward. The wolf went flying into the air.

This time, the chicken had his thunder ready.

KRA-KOOWWWW!

The wolf landed and rolled, then scrambled to its feet. It tried to look tough, but that second bolt had hit its soft underbelly. Its eyes peered in different directions, one of them half-shut, and its tongue dangled sideways from its mouth.

It wobbled one way, stumbled the other, and finally sat down and howled.

"How-OOOOooOOOooool..."

With a puff of smoke, the wolf was gone.

"Bad dog," Brunhilde said. "No chicken for you."

Olga, Sven, and the rest of the chickens came out. The storm clouds parted, and the morning was bright again.

"You were so brave," Olga said, patting Thundercluck's helmet.

"The other chickens wouldn't even watch out the window!" said Sven.

Hennda fluttered to Thundercluck and put her wings around him.

Sven crouched to pick up his weather vane, which had been warped by the wolf's magic blast. Its eyes had once looked bored. Now they looked surprised.

Sven glanced at the rest of the flock, then said to Brunhilde, "Thank you for keeping us safe."

"Thank *you*," she replied, "for keeping *him* safe." She gave Thundercluck a playful thump on the shoulder. "I'll take it from here."

The chickens still stared at Thundercluck, but no longer with disdain. Now they looked at him with awe. One waddled up and dropped a worm at his feet.

"Well, that's awful nice," Brunhilde said, "but, uh ... we've got to go. Come,

Thundercluck! Come, Hennda! Asgard awaits. Let's get you home!"

In a faraway realm, a torch flickered in a shadowy room. The wolf crept into sight. It bowed before a hooded figure sitting on a kitchen stool.

"Sit," said the figure, and the wolf obeyed. "Roll over." The wolf turned belly up, and with a skeletal hand, the figure plucked a feather from its fur.

The figure's mustache curled in a grin. From his frying pan he drew a bone, which he tossed into the shadows. The wolf scrambled after it.

"Begone, you mongrel," the figure said. "Your work for me is done. Now . . ."

Gorman Bones rose to his feet and held up his frying pan.

". . . let's get cooking."

CHAPTER 7
GOLDEN BIRD

WITH BRUNHILDE LEADING THE WAY,
Thundercluck and his mother rode the rainbow to Asgard. The light faded as they landed on the Bifrost.

Hennda gazed at her old home. To her, this felt like the end of a long trip. To Thundercluck, it felt like the start of something wonderful.

An ocean shimmered in the east. In the west was the kingdom, a glittering domain of golden towers. Mountains loomed beyond, and the Castle of Asgard rose above them, radiant in the afternoon sun. Thundercluck was mesmerized.

"Greetings!" a voice boomed. A red-bearded fellow wearing a cape was running their way. Hennda squawked and fluttered to his shoulder. Thundercluck could do nothing but gape, especially at the hammer hooked on his belt.

Brunhilde patted the chicken's wing. "That's Thor," she whispered. "You'll like him."

"Welcome back," Thor said. He looked at Brunhilde's injured wing and asked, "Eventful trip?"

"Nothing we couldn't handle," Brunhilde said with a smile.

The god smiled back and turned to the chickens. "Hennda," he said, "your coop awaits, just as you left it. Your journey has been long, and your son is in good hands."

Hennda nuzzled Thundercluck. Then she flew off. Her flight was wobbly—her wings had been out of practice for years—but Thundercluck was shocked. He had never known his mother could fly. She turned to wink at him and flapped out of sight.

"Now, young heroes," Thor said. Thundercluck had never been called that, but he liked the feel of it. "We must consult with Odin, but the kingdom cannot know you've returned." He unpinned his cape and threw it over Thundercluck's head.

Brunhilde fashioned the cape as a cloak around the bird. "It's a chicken wrap," she said.

"Now, to Mount Fjell!" said the god.

Brunhilde whispered to Thundercluck, "That means we're going through the market."

Thor led them through the Market of Asgard. Thundercluck trotted behind, and it was all he could do not to stop and gawk. Sellers beckoned from tables and tents, all lined with potions, trinkets, and jewels.

The Castle of Asgard towered above them, closer now. Brunhilde pointed toward it with her sword. "That's the home of the gods," she said. "They live for thousands of years, and their magic is so strong, it flows into all the realms."

Thor looked over his shoulder with a smile and gave his hammer a twirl.

Brunhilde gestured to the market and said, "The other Asgardians are villagers, all spell-casters and craftspeople. They make the realm shine, and they share their magic here." Thundercluck read some of the market's banners.

Mystic Merum's Truth Serum: Results You Can Trust!

Thrifty Max's Battle-Axes: Break Your Enemies, Not the Bank!

Frizzy Pat's Wizard Hats: You Shall Not Pass...On These Bargains!

Everyone's so different here, thought Thundercluck, *but somehow, I feel right at home.* Frizzy Pat gave a friendly nod their way.

The chicken also noticed that everywhere he looked, Asgardians were eating golden apples. Brunhilde nodded and said, "Yup, we sure do love apples. But look! We're coming to the mountains."

They had reached the market's edge, where a trail rose into the mountain range. Thor pointed with his hammer and said, "We must summit Mount Fjell, the tallest peak before us. How's that wing, Battle Maiden?"

Brunhilde gave a flap and said, "Better by the minute."

"Fly on, then," Thor said, "and I'll meet you there soon. Odin awaits!"

Thundercluck and Brunhilde flew up Mount Fjell. They went slowly, as Brunhilde was still recovering and Thundercluck was new to flight. They found King Odin at the summit. He stood quietly, gazing at the plains below.

With his eye still on the fields, Odin called, "All is peaceful now, but we stand on the brink of a great battle." He turned to them. "Well met, Brunhilde ... and greetings, golden bird!"

Thundercluck was still wrapped in Thor's cape, but Odin's eye seemed to pierce through its folds.

"Brunhilde brought you here through the Bifrost," the elder god said, "but that is not the only way between realms. By some dark magic, monsters have come to this world, and soon they shall gather upon these plains."

Two ravens flew into view. Odin held up a hand and called, "Huginn! Muninn!" The ravens landed on his wrist.

"Ca-caw! Ca-caw!" they cried.

"Yes, yes, I see," Odin said. He looked at the heroes.

"My ravens bring news of the enemy, whose forces are peppered with orcs, goblins, gremlins ... and man-pigs."

Brunhilde groaned. Thundercluck cocked his head.

"Man-pigs are a new blight upon the realms," Odin said. "They walk like men, but oink like pigs, and their souls are as twisted as their tails."

"Ca-caw!" the ravens repeated.

"Mmm," said Odin. "They tell of two monsters who tower above all others. We know not what they are, but their shadows are long, and their footsteps shake the ground. Tomorrow we shall learn what devils await."

Brunhilde asked, "You got all that from 'Ca-caw'?"

"My son approaches!" Odin said, and Thor climbed onto the summit.

The Thunder God carried two bags. Wheezing, he handed them to Brunhilde and said, "These are your tents." He wiped sweat from his brow and muttered, "I'm better at moving mountains than climbing them."

"Tents?" Brunhilde asked.

"When the enemy invades," Odin said, "this is where they'll come: the Valley of Dal." He pointed to the valley below, which passed through the mountains toward the castle. "Saga foretells our army will struggle, so we want the two of you to watch."

Thor took his cape back from Thundercluck. He wiped his brow and said, "We will hide a squadron of warriors behind this mountain. If you see our main forces are in danger, you must fly to the hidden squadron for help."

"Oh," said Brunhilde.

"Thor and I must go now," Odin said. "We will gather our warriors in Valhalla. Arise at dawn, for that is when we make our stand."

That night, Thundercluck and Brunhilde camped on the summit. They sat by a campfire, listening to crickets and looking at stars. From the kingdom below, they heard Valhalla's army cheer.

"I thought I was starting to prove myself," Brunhilde said.

Thundercluck blinked and said, "Ba-gerk?"

"All I get is guard duty and messenger jobs," she said. Then she smiled and added, "But at least I got to bring you home."

Thundercluck leaned his head against her.

"We used to have slumber parties when we were little," she said. "Do you remember any of that?"

The chicken scrunched his brow, but all he could remember was the farm.

"Maybe it'll come back. For now, let's get some rest. It's been a big day, and tomorrow's going to be even bigger!"

Thundercluck thought he might be too excited to sleep, but exhaustion soon took over. As he drifted off, words from the day echoed in his mind: *Magic. Hero. Monsters. Danger.*

And just before he slept, he thought of Brunhilde and one more word: *Friend.*

CHAPTER 8
THE BATTLE OF DAL

THUNDERCLUCK AND BRUNHILDE WOKE
at dawn. They could see Valhalla's army below. At its front stood Thor with his hammer. Odin sat astride his eight-legged horse. In the morning's first rays, the enemy approached: a mass of man-pigs.

"Charge!" cried Odin, and Valhalla's army surged.

Thundercluck and Brunhilde watched the armies clash. At first the battle went well. The gods, the Valkyries, and the Vikings fought valiantly, pushing the pigs back.

But then, from behind two mountains, the monsters appeared.

Brunhilde recognized them from her studies: they were the ice giantess Frostiik and the fire dragon Blimpor. Throughout the realms, Frostiik's breath had frozen villages into ice, while Blimpor's fire breath had set towns ablaze. Each was devastating alone, but never before had they teamed up.

"What treachery is this?" Odin yelled.

The monsters' approach was slow, but menacing. The giantess lumbered with bone-shaking steps, and the floating, gassy dragon batted its wings.

THUD...Flap, flap...THUD...Flap, flap...THUD... Flap, flap...

Thor broke from the main battle to face the beasts. He held his hammer high.

BA-ZOWWWW!

A blinding bolt of lightning hit the dragon.

Wow, thought Thundercluck, *that's a lot more power than I have!*

The dragon was shaken, but not slain. Thor prepared to strike again.

WHOOSH!

Frostiik's breath rushed over the god, freezing his hand and hammer in a block of ice. Thor was pinned.

"They need help," Brunhilde said. "Let's launch plan B: the hidden troops!"

She and Thundercluck turned to the other side of the mountain, but their hearts sank. Man-pigs had surrounded Mount Fjell, and the hidden troops were already busy in battle.

Turning back, the pair saw Thor struggling to escape

the ice, but it held fast. Blimpor hovered closer, preparing to scorch the god.

Brunhilde looked at Thundercluck. "We've got to do something!"

The chicken gulped.

FWOOOOM!

Blimpor unleashed his fire. A figure dropped in front of Thor in a blur, just as flames began to engulf him. Valhalla's army gaped in fear.

The fiery wave parted to reveal Brunhilde. She crouched in front of Thor, her shield casting a protective dome around herself and the god.

Frostiik inhaled, ready to blast the god again with ice.
BOOM! KRA-KOWWW!

Thundercluck hit both monsters with lightning bolts. The beasts were startled—and angry. They glared at the chicken.

Brunhilde smacked her sword against the ice imprisoning Thor, but she barely chipped it. Thor tilted his head toward the monsters and said, "Help Thundercluck!"

The Battle Maiden slashed with her blade. An arc of light hit the giantess. "Hey, you!" Brunhilde called. "Catch me if you can!" She took flight.

Frostiik chased Brunhilde, leaving Thundercluck with Blimpor. The bird hit the dragon with bolt after bolt, but the beast endured and spat fireballs in return. Thundercluck spiraled around them. He prepared to launch another bolt, but he was starting to tire.

"Thundercluck, wait!" Brunhilde called. She ducked under a blast of ice and flew to the chicken. "I'm not having much luck, either," she said. Her teeth chattered, and frost covered part of her armor. "They're immune to our magic, and they don't have soft spots!"

Thundercluck looked worried, but Brunhilde reassured him. "They're tough, but we're fast. Follow my lead!"

She flapped upward, and Thundercluck followed. The monsters kept belching ice and fire, and every time their attacks crossed, the collision burst into steam. Soon they were all surrounded by thick, puffy clouds.

"Now they can only see a few feet ahead!" Brunhilde shouted. "You fly so the dragon can see you, and I'll do the same with the giantess. When you hear my call, come toward the sound of my voice. Let's go!"

The heroes split, and when Thundercluck got close enough, he wiggled his tail in the dragon's face. Blimpor roared a fiery blast. The chicken whirled aside, and then he heard Brunhilde shout, "Now, Thundercluck! To me!"

He swooped in a backflip, and Blimpor chased him with his fire breath. With Frostiik at her heels,

Brunhilde caught Thundercluck in midflight and guarded him with her shield. Flames soared above them. An icy gust flew beneath. Two roars erupted so loudly that all the steam blew away.

Both armies stopped fighting to look. As the smoke cleared, everyone saw Frostiik and Blimpor spinning in distress. The dragon's rump was frozen, and the giantess's loincloth was on fire. They had breathed fire and ice on each other.

Each monster tried to blow on its own rear, but neither one could reach it. They howled as they fled, the giantess's loincloth leaving a trail of smoke in the air and the dragon's behind frosting the grassy plain as it passed.

"Retreat!" cried the biggest man-pig. "Retreeeeaaaaat!"

The word echoed through the battlefield, and soon the whole horde had dispersed. Valhalla's army cheered. Thor's ice block thawed, and the god broke free.

Across the plain, Brunhilde caught Odin's eye. She shrugged as if to say, *Sorry we broke the rules . . . and saved everybody's lives.* The elder god nodded silently.

"Ba-bwak?" Thundercluck inquired.

"I think that means we're heroes," Brunhilde said. "But we also might be grounded."

In another realm, under a blistering sky, a giant volcano smoldered. Deep within a cave, Gorman Bones sat hunched on his kitchen stool.

He snapped his skeletal fingers, and a rush of smoke came swirling up. The cloud parted, and in

its wake stood the man-pig who had ordered the retreat. He bowed with a bashful snort.

"Captain War-Tog," said the Cook. "Tell me, how did the battle go?"

"Uh, B-Boss," War-Tog stammered, "we—we woulda won, Boss, but... but they had this pair of warriors, a Valkyrie and a chicken—"

"A *chicken*, you say?" Gorman leaned forward with a grin. "Well then, everything is going as planned."

War-Tog blinked. "You ... You're not mad, Boss?"

"Mad?" The Cook rose from his stool, and from his apron's pocket he lifted *The Recipe Book of the Dead*. "Mad with anticipation, perhaps. And soon ... mad with power!"

Gorman began to chuckle, then he threw his head back with a cackle. War-Tog looked confused, but he started to laugh, too. "Good ... Good one, Boss," the man-pig chuckled.

"I know!" barked the Cook, and the laughter stopped immediately. "Now," he went on, "it's time to make something sinister, but sweet."

War-Tog nodded enthusiastically.

"And once it's ready," Gorman concluded, "I'll serve Asgard my revenge."

CHAPTER 9
HOME TO ROOST

IN THE WEEKS THAT FOLLOWED, Thundercluck and Brunhilde became celebrities in Asgard. Saga's warning faded from memory, and the kingdom welcomed the chicken's return.

For disobeying orders, the heroes' only punishment was to wash the palace dishes. This led to the greatest bubble fight the realm had ever known. When the suds were wiped away, the castle shone like never before.

Ballads were sung and tapestries hung to honor the duo's glory. In the market, Frizzy Pat sold wizard hats

inspired by their helmets. From the castle to Valhalla to the Asgardian Historic District, fans met the heroes with gratitude. Thundercluck and Brunhilde kept busy, always shaking hands and kissing babies.

Away from the crowds, the friends remained inseparable. They explored the palace grounds and played dress-up in the castle closets. When they hosted a tea party in Valhalla, all the gods attended. Even Odin— always so serious and grim—came with a fancy bib and teacup.

Everywhere they went, Thundercluck saw statues of birds and wings. Even the staircase to the Catacombs had a crow made of iron on its railing. For the first time he could remember, Thundercluck felt like he was home.

One peaceful day, Thor called Thundercluck to the fields. The god had arranged two wooden man-pigs under a sign that read POWER TRAINING. Thundercluck cocked his head, and Thor said, "Come with me, my feathered friend."

They walked until the targets were almost out of sight.

"You have talent," the Thunder God said, "but do you have skill? Try to strike a target from here."

Thundercluck squinted and launched a bolt. It shot through the air, but over the distance it weakened, fizzling out before its goal.

"You must practice," Thor said, raising his hammer at the targets, "and focus. Keep in mind what matters most." Lightning erupted from the hammer and blasted both targets to ash.

The chicken's beak fell open.

"Make no mistake, I am proud of you," Thor said. "You have prevailed in battle—but how much of that is thanks to Brunhilde? If you find yourself without her, can you stand alone?"

Thundercluck looked at the ground.

Thor placed a finger under Thundercluck's beak and lifted his gaze. "I ask because I care," he said, "and I know you have great potential."

Thus began Thundercluck's training. Over the weeks, he learned not only to control his bolts, but also to heed his instincts, to hear the bagaws within. He came to trust Thor with every feather of his being.

One day during practice, a horn sounded from the castle. "My father calls you," Thor said. "Find him on the castle's highest balcony."

Thundercluck flew to the balcony. He found King Odin and Queen Frigg looking out upon the realm.

Frigg turned to him and said, "Greetings, hero. You have proved yourself vital to our kingdom. Long have we wondered what to tell you of your past...and what to foretell of your future."

Thundercluck cocked his head.

"What lies ahead," Odin said, "is yours to discover, but we must warn you of your greatest foe: the grim chef Gorman Bones."

That name was new to Thundercluck, but his heart skipped a beat. Then he felt a presence behind him and turned.

In the balcony's doorway stood Saga.

Thundercluck had heard of this goddess—the ethereal fortune-teller—but this was the first time he could remember seeing her in person. In her eyes he saw wisdom and compassion. She placed her hand upon his cheek and spoke:

You fight with honor, Thundercluck;
your glory has begun.
But gird your loins and chicken bits—
the worst is yet to come.

An evil chef is plotting with a diabolic book;
You'll need your courage, and your wits,
to face the Under-Cook.

Thundercluck shuddered, but then he shook his head and tried to look brave. He bowed to the goddess and said, "Buk-bwok."

Brunhilde isn't scared of anything, he thought, *and neither am I! I'm the Chicken of Thor. What could go wrong?*

Months passed peacefully, and the heroes kept training. "Next time evil comes our way," Brunhilde said, "we'll whup it even better than before!"

Thundercluck's twelfth birthday came, and Valhalla honored him with a feast. The good chef Andy made cake for all, and he served the bird a shiny plate of seeds. Thundercluck perched at the head of a table with Brunhilde and Thor beside him. Hennda, Odin, and Frigg sat nearby. Everyone came to celebrate, except Saga, who was not much of a party person.

"A toast!" Thor shouted, tapping his hammer on his goblet. "To the rooster of the hour; to the bird with the bolts—to the hero Thundercluck!"

"TO THE HERO THUNDERCLUCK!" cheered the crowd.

But then a deathly chill descended.

Well, well," a disembodied voice called out. Thundercluck's blood ran cold. "Doesn't this look *scrumptious*. Mind if I join you for dessert?"

Valhalla went dark with smoke. The Asgardians started coughing, but then a gust of wind cleared the air. The hall's doors swung open, and there stood a skeleton with an apron, a mustache, and a cook's hat.

"Gorman," Thor growled, rising from his seat. "You look thin."

"Please," replied the Cook as fire danced in the sockets of his skull, "call me Bones."

CHAPTER 10
FROZEN CHICKEN

"HOW LONG HAS IT BEEN SINCE LAST I was here?" Gorman Bones asked. He looked at the banner that read, HAPPY TWELFTH BIRTHDAY, THUNDER-CLUCK.

"Oh, of course," the Cook said. "Twelve years." He turned to Thundercluck and added, *"To the day."*

He eyed the cake and mused, "Hmm, when I said 'scrumptious' . . . perhaps I was too kind. What was the goal with this cake? Low sugar? Low fat? Low flavor?" He grinned at Asgard's chef. "No offense, Andhrímnir."

An awkward silence followed, but Brunhilde broke it. "I think Andy's cake is great," she said, "and just adding 'no offense' doesn't make you any less of a jer—"

"Silence, petulant child!" Gorman barked. Brunhilde held his gaze and slowly folded her arms. The Cook cleared his throat. "Now, where was I? Ah yes, this cake is terrible. But worry not, Asgardians...I've brought you all a treat."

"We'll eat no food of yours," Thor grunted. "Anything you'd serve is cursed!"

"Oh, yes," Bones answered, "it's cursed, all right, but you'll eat it just the same. Each and every one of you! After all, who could say no...to homemade apple pie?" The Cook snapped his fingers, and with poofs of smoke, slices of pie appeared on everyone's plates.

Everyone gasped. Asgardians hated evil...but they loved apple pie.

Odin stood and glared at Gorman. "Listen well, Under-Cook," he said. "My kingdom will not be tempted by...Is that...Is that nutmeg I smell?"

"Just a pinch," the Cook replied. "Enough to enrich the flavor, but not overpower it. Go ahead. Try it."

A glazed look came over Odin's eyes. He sat back down . . . and started eating his pie. Queen Frigg did the same, and one by one, the other Asgardians followed suit. Thundercluck's eyes widened. Odin had warned him the Cook was dangerous, but everyone was eating his pie.

"We must stop eating!" cried Thor, his mouth overflowing as he shoveled in more pie. "This pie must be cursed! But I . . . can't stop . . . It's too delicious!"

Even Andy ate his piece, and Hennda pecked at her own little slice. But no pie had appeared for Thundercluck, and at his side, Brunhilde was the only Asgardian not digging in. Everyone else had been enticed by the apple smell, but Brunhilde was holding her nose.

Gorman did not notice. He only had eyes for the chicken. "So sorry I couldn't offer the pie to *you*, birthday bird," he said, striding forward with his frying pan. "But I have plans for you, and after all, I must keep my ingredients . . . fresh."

One by one, the Asgardians fell asleep where they

sat. Soon the only pie eater still awake was Thor, who blurted out, "Gorman Bones has cursed us all!" before falling facedown onto his plate. The Thunder God snored so loudly it shook the table.

That's it, thought Thundercluck. *Time to zap the Cook!* He jumped from his perch and blasted out a lightning bolt, but the chef whipped up his frying pan to block it. To Thundercluck's surprise, the pan absorbed the bolt, then sizzled and glowed red.

The Cook waved the pan in the air, and it erupted with fire, smoke, and lightning bolts.

Thundercluck's stomach dropped. The bird had known that some could resist his thunder, but this

was the first time anyone had absorbed it and grown stronger.

Gorman Bones lowered his pan with a toothy grin. Thundercluck felt frozen in place. He wanted to squawk, he wanted to fight, he wanted to run ... but all he could do was stand and quiver.

"Yes, good chicken," Gorman whispered, striding closer. "Stay still, and I'll have you battered in no time." He raised his pan and swung at the bird.

CLANG!

Inches from Thundercluck's head, the pan came to a stop against Brunhilde's blade. She bellowed, "YOU LEAVE MY FRIEND ALONE!"

Gorman's eyes darted to the girl's plate, where her slice of pie sat with a fork jabbed in it.

"I'll stick with birthday cake," she snarled.

The chef looked at his pan, which now had a notch cut where the sword had hit it. "How dare you interfere," he grumbled. Then he leapt back and cried, "Guards!"

Thundercluck flew to a distant rafter, and an

entourage of man-pigs—four in total—shuffled through the open doors. They formed a row between the girl and the Cook. The biggest pig grunted, and Gorman commanded, "Captain War-Tog! You and your fellow swine keep the girl at bay . . . I need a word with the bird."

The chef crept backward, and the pigs glared at Brunhilde. One of them sneered, "I bet she's not so tough without the chicken!"

Brunhilde's sword began to glow. "Tell me, pigs— do you know why a Valkyrie is called a Battle Maiden?"

War-Tog snorted, and said, "No. Why?"

Brunhilde smiled as her helmet's visor clinked down. "Well, piggy," she said, "you're about to learn."

"Heeere, chicken-chicken," Gorman called to the ceiling. Thundercluck's talons held fast to the rafter. "I see you up there," the Cook hissed.

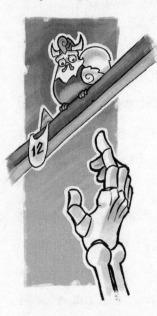

An axe clattered at the chef's feet, and he stepped aside as a man-pig flew by and tumbled to the floor. The pig lay still and groaned.

Across the room, Brunhilde shot a quick look at the Cook, then focused back on War-Tog and the other two pigs.

Gorman glanced at the fallen hog, then looked up at the rafter. "Your friend is putting up a fight," he said. "I can't reach you ... Why don't you come down and play?" He brandished his pan, and flames trailed behind it.

Thundercluck shifted from one foot to the other, but his wings felt stuck to his sides. He tried to flap, but all he could do was twitch.

"Very well," sighed the chef. Another axe flew by, this time wedging itself in a chair, and a second man-pig went rolling into the first.

Gorman stepped over the wheezing pigs and strolled through the dining hall. He traced his fingers over nearby Asgardians as they slept. "If I can't have the Bird of Thunder," he said, stopping behind Thor, "then I'll settle for the god." And with a grunt, he lifted Thor onto his shoulder.

Thundercluck's brows bent in rage. He managed a timid squawk, but still he stayed shaking on the rafter.

"Oh, does that upset you, chicken?" The chef looked back at the bird. "He's like the father you never had, isn't he? Well, you *could* come down to save him."

Thundercluck's heart pounded in his chest. He wanted so badly to move, but he remembered the frying pan and its terrible blaze. His eyes were locked on Thor. All he could do was tremble.

Brunhilde slashed with her blade, and its magic sent the remaining two pigs flying. From midair, War-Tog shouted, "Sorry, Boss!"

Brunhilde turned to the chef and called, "Hey, mustache! You're next!"

She charged his way, but Gorman held his gaze on Thundercluck. "Last chance!" he whispered, and with his free hand he held his pan high. When Brunhilde was almost upon him, he swung the pan down, and a cloud of smoke burst at his feet.

Brunhilde ran coughing through the smoke, but the Cook had already vanished. So, too, had the man-pigs and Thor.

Faint snores echoed through Valhalla. Asgard's young heroes were alone.

"Thundercluck!" Brunhilde called. "Are you okay?"

The chicken could only blink.

Brunhilde looked around. "It's safe. He's gone . . . You can come down."

Thundercluck exhaled. At last, his wings would move again. He squawked and fluttered to Brunhilde. The terror in his chest had faded. Shame had taken its place.

Brunhilde hugged him and said, "I'm glad you're okay!" She looked around. "We have to do something," she said. "Every single Asgardian was here . . . except Saga! She wanted me to tell you happy birthday, but she likes her personal space. She'll know what to do. To the Seeing Throne!"

They sprinted through the castle, running by the Catacombs staircase with its sculpted crow on the railing. *I can't believe it*, Thundercluck thought. *I just stood there! But maybe Saga can make things right . . .*

"Here we are!" Brunhilde shouted. The chamber's curtain was closed. "Saga's behind there, and she'll know what to do!"

Brunhilde drew aside the curtain and whispered, "Oh no."

The Goddess of Vision and Foresight sat slumped in her throne, an empty plate on her lap. Little pieces of pie were stuck to her cheeks and mouth. Her eyes were closed, and her breathing was slow and even.

"Saga!" Brunhilde said. "Saga, are you awake?"

The fortune-teller's eyes fluttered open, and with difficulty she said:

> *That pie appeared before me, dear,*
> *by some unholy stealth . . .*
> *I knew that it was evil, but . . . I couldn't help myself.*
> *Beware of Gorman's dining hall, his vile dinner venue.*
> *Now, find the mystic travel book, or doom is on the menu!*

The goddess yawned and closed her eyes. She started snoring.

After a moment, Brunhilde poked Saga's shoulder, and her eyes flew open for one last shout:

Yes, DOOM! It falls upon us all, unless we break this curse.

The Cook must be defeated soon; the spell must be reversed.

There's treachery ahead, you two.

We need you at your bravest,

For Asgard's fate is in your hands . . .

and only you can save us.

PART III

THUNDERCLUCK TRAVELS

CHAPTER 11
THE JOURNEY BEGINS

THUNDERCLUCK STARED AT SAGA AS SHE slept. The chicken lowered his head and wished he could disappear under his helmet.

Brunhilde stayed quiet for a moment, but then said, "Well, you heard the lady. Let's move!" Determination glowed in her eyes, but she softened when she saw Thundercluck staring at his feet.

"Look," she said, "I know this is bad, but we can make it better. Saga said to find a travel book, so let's check the library."

They entered the Asgardian Hall of Books, dark

and quiet in the night. Starlight fell through the windows, and shadows loomed among the bookshelves.

Brunhilde grabbed a candle from the reception desk. She held it out to Thundercluck and said, "Can you light this?"

Thundercluck looked at the candle. He pointed his wing and tried to zap it . . . but nothing happened. Earlier he had felt fully charged, but now he felt empty. He felt like something inside him was missing.

"Hmm," said Brunhilde. "I . . . How about I just make my sword glow."

The heroes wandered, and Brunhilde read the shelves' categories as they went. "Transcendence, Transmutation . . . ah, here we go! Travel."

On the Travel shelf sat a treasure chest with a golden lock.

"That looks special," Brunhilde said, "but we don't have a key." She looked closely at the lock, where an inscription read:

NO MAGIC OR SHOCK CAN OPEN THIS LOCK.

NO WEAPON CAN DAMAGE THIS THING.

BUT BIRDS OF A FEATHER CAN JOURNEY TOGETHER.

THE SECRET IS UNDER YOUR WING.

While the heroes pondered the riddle, a feather fell from Brunhilde's wing. Thundercluck picked it up with his beak. He caught Brunhilde's eye, and they both looked from the feather to the keyhole. Brunhilde took the feather and slid it into the lock. The chest opened to reveal a book called *Magic and Stones May Carry Me Home: The Travels of S. Valkamor.*

Thundercluck cocked his head as Brunhilde opened the book. Flipping through the pages, she whistled and said, "Whoever S. Valkamor was, they did a lot of sightseeing! And had a thing for poetry." She stopped on a dog-eared page, which read:

TO THE ROOTS (A VALKAMOR VERSE)

When mystery calls, an elder knows all,
A watcher you seldom can see.
If tidings are bleak, if wisdom you seek,
Then go to the roots of the tree.

Thundercluck remembered the tree on the tapestry in Olga and Sven's basement. *Egg-dra-sill*, he thought.

"Yggdrasil," Brunhilde whispered.

When the word was spoken, the book's pages fluttered on their own. They stopped on a page with a section torn off and a poem that read:

TO THE STONES (A VALKAMOR VERSE)

With cunning and haste, with magic and grace,
The stones will deliver you there.
And now I bequeath you, the first is beneath you,
So go to the crow on the stairs.

Brunhilde looked at Thundercluck and said, "So, we're supposed to get to Yggdrasil . . . using rocks? And great, part of the page is missing." She remembered her studies. "The Bifrost only goes to Earth and back. Some wizards can teleport with spells, but that's not magic you and I can do."

Thundercluck looked at his wings. He felt hollow inside.

"Whatever these 'stones' are, I guess we have to find them," Brunhilde said.

Thundercluck reread the poem. *The first is beneath you, so go to the crow on the stairs.*

Brunhilde closed the book and put it in her Battle Bag. It fit perfectly.

"We need to hurry," she said, turning to a nearby window. "Come look; there's something important in the sky."

She pointed outside, and Thundercluck saw ribbons of color stretching across the dark night.

"Did Sven and Olga ever show you this? In Midgard, people call it the Northern Lights," Brunhilde said. "It's Asgardian magic; we call it the Aurora." She pointed with her sword and asked, "Do you see those stars?"

The chicken saw a line of stars shining brightly in a row.

"When Asgard's in danger," Brunhilde went on, "the Aurora protects the kingdom. No one can attack while it's on, but it only lasts nine days."

Thundercluck counted the stars. There were nine.

"We'll be able to see those from every realm," Brunhilde said. "With each new sunrise, a star will twinkle out. We have to break the curse before all nine fade, or Asgard's magic will be lost forever."

The chicken gulped.

Brunhilde smiled and asked, "Think we can do it in time?"

Nine days? Thundercluck thought.

"Absolutely," Brunhilde said with a wink. "Now, let's find some stones. Where should we start?"

Thundercluck remembered Brunhilde's tour of Asgard. He thought about dress-up in the castle closets, the tea party in Valhalla . . . and the iron crow on the Catacombs staircase.

"Buk-bwak!" he said, and he trotted in that direction. Brunhilde followed.

On the way to the Catacombs, Brunhilde grabbed her emergency backpacks from her room. Their tags said, TRAGIC JACK'S MAGIC PACKS: I'VE GOT BAGGAGE!

"These contain all the food and camping supplies we'll need," she explained.

The duo crept down the crow-marked staircase, and Brunhilde lit her sword as they entered the Catacombs. These were narrow tunnels under the castle, caves even darker than the library. Brunhilde's sword could only shine so far, leaving shadows lurking in every corner.

Brunhilde kicked some crumbly dust aside and whispered, "Back when Gorman was our chef, he was working on a recipe for magic muffins. *Bran* muffins." She shivered. "He was always making a mess, and he stashed his work down here in the Catacombs."

Thundercluck was already nervous, and thinking about Gorman made it worse.

"After Gorman vanished," Brunhilde went on, "Thor came down to clean up the mess he'd left behind. Thor said he cleared all the muffins out...but you never know with bran muffins."

They came to a spiderweb, and Brunhilde stopped. "A few years later," she said, "Loki the trickster had a little pet spider, and he set it loose down here as part of some prank. I guess it's still alive." She started forward again and added, "Keep your eyes open for that spider... It was itsy-bitsy, so look closely."

Thundercluck turned and looked over his tail. *Maybe we should go back*, he thought. *Maybe if we go to sleep, we'll wake up tomorrow and everything will be fine.* Then he told himself, *No. Our problems won't fix themselves.*

Brunhilde peeked around a corner and said, "Oh look. There's the spider." Then her helmet's visor dropped into battle mode, and she added, "It's not itsy-bitsy anymore."

Thundercluck's eyes whipped forward. The spider towered over them. After years of feeding on forgotten bran muffins, it had bloated to gargantuan size. It stood taller than Brunhilde, and its hairy legs sprawled across the tunnel.

In the light of Brunhilde's sword, the spider's eight eyes glinted with fury.

Brunhilde whispered, "I don't think it likes us . . . but look!" With her sword she pointed beyond the beast to a stone on a platform.

"Listen, spider," she shouted, "we need to get to that stone! Will you let us pass?"

The spider made a rattling, hissing noise and reared up, pressing its head against the tunnel's ceiling.

"All right," Brunhilde said, "we tried asking nicely. Thundercluck! How about you give this thing a jolt? . . . Thundercluck?"

She turned to the bird, but he was frozen stiff. His eyes darted from her to the spider and back again.

The spider screeched and poked a hairy leg at Thundercluck. Brunhilde yelled, "It's trying to grab you!" then swatted the leg away with her shield. The chicken stood still, and the spider crept forward.

"Not so fast," Brunhilde said. She lowered her sword, and for a moment everything went dark. Then a flash of light slashed through the black. The spider shrieked and ducked. The magic hit the tunnel ceiling, and all was dark again. The only sound was falling rocks.

Brunhilde lit her sword again. She spotted the spider scuttling away through a hole she had blasted in the ceiling.

Beyond the rubble, the stone awaited, its surface marked with mystic symbols. Though the Catacombs

were pitch-dark, flowers grew at the stone's base.
Among the flowers was a ragged piece of paper.

"The missing part of the page!" Brunhilde said. She
picked it up and read, "Rune-stone instructions: 1) Strike
with magic. 2) Step on platform. 3) Adventure."

Adventure . . . and magic, Thundercluck thought.
He shuffled his feet. They needed to activate the
stone, but his magic was gone. Brunhilde looked at

him and lifted her visor. Her eyes twinkled with concern.

It quickly vanished, though, and she clinked her visor back down. "We'll get your thunder back," she said, "but for now, I'll handle this."

She slashed a wave of light onto the stone, which sounded with a CLANG!

The runes began to glow, bathing the pair in an emerald light.

Brunhilde sniffed and said, "It smells like there's a garden ahead. Let's go!"

Thundercluck lingered. *I can't do this*, he thought. *I don't know what's out there, and I don't have my powers! Maybe I can get back to the farm where I grew up . . . I'd be safe there.*

Brunhilde turned to face him. "Hey," she said, "I know this is scary. I'm not going to make you do anything you don't want to, but"—she lifted her visor again—"you're my best friend. I hope you'll come with me."

The chicken took a deep breath. *You're my best friend, too*, he thought. He stepped forward.

Brunhilde lowered her visor with a smile. She took Thundercluck's wing in her hand, and together they stood on the platform. With a flash of green light, they were gone.

CHAPTER 12
ACROSS THE REALMS

WAVES OF MAGIC SWIRLED AROUND THE heroes. The light faded, and a night sky came into view.

"This is Alfheim, the realm of gardens," Brunhilde said.

They stood on a rune-stone surrounded by flowers. It smelled like nectar and spring. The moon hung high in the sky, but brighter light shone from small, colorful orbs near the ground.

One floated toward the heroes, and when it had neared, they saw it was a little glowing person. It had butterfly wings and wore a leaf as a tunic.

Brunhilde leaned close to Thundercluck's ear and whispered, "Fair folk." She raised her hand, and the fairy landed on her knuckle. Brunhilde cleared her throat. "Greetings, fairy! We come from Asgard on a holy quest. We arrived by rune-stone." She gestured to the stone. "Do you know where we might find another?"

The fairy smiled and said, "I like flowers!"

"Okay, thank you," Brunhilde said, and the fairy flew away. Brunhilde said to Thundercluck, "Looks like we'll need to figure this out ourselves. Tonight, let's camp here."

The chicken tossed, turned, and clucked as he slept. He dreamed he was running from the Under-Cook, and no matter how he flapped his wings, he was too weak to fly. He looked over his shoulder, and the Cook's pan burst into thunder and flame.

In his tent, Thundercluck squawked, and his eyes shot open. His heart was pounding, but slowly he calmed himself. It was still dark out. The garden was tranquil. The chicken's terror faded, but the thought remained: *That Cook is still out there.*

The bird poked his head out of his tent. Brunhilde sat nearby, inspecting the book by the light of her sword. She looked his way.

"This thing's full of riddles," she said, closing the book. "Let's get some rest. We'll need it."

The sun rose, and the heroes watched a star twinkle out. Eight remained. Brunhilde opened the Valkamor travel book, whose pages flew open again to the same poem.

"Let's see if we can find a clue," Brunhilde said. Thundercluck looked around. He saw flowers, streams, and lots of bushes. Four of the largest bushes, shaped like animals, were scattered in different directions: a horse, a duck, a rabbit, and a fox.

"Hmm. Yesterday the book flipped to a page when I said 'Yggdrasil.' Now we're in Alfheim, so—"

When the realm's name was spoken, the pages flipped again. The book settled on a new poem.

THROUGH ALFHEIM (A HAIKU)

The hopping bush waits
And feels the breath of winter.
It comes from the rose.

"So," Brunhilde said, "there's a hopping bush, apparently." She looked at the plants surrounding them, all firmly rooted to the ground. "None of these are exactly jumping."

Thundercluck squinted at the bushes shaped like animals, particularly the rabbit. He pointed and said, "Buk buk?"

"Maybe you're on to something," Brunhilde said. "Let's see!"

They flew to the hedge, which sat on the bank of a stream. A small group of fairies hovered there.

"Greetings," Brunhilde said. "We seek—"

"I'm cold!" one of the fairies said. "It's cold that way!" He pointed upstream.

"All right, thanks." Brunhilde turned to Thundercluck. "I think that actually does help. Let's check it out!"

The heroes flew upstream. Behind them the realm was warm, but the air became colder as they went. They stopped where the water was frozen along the bank. "Look," Brunhilde said.

Beside the stream and beneath a tree was a patch of snow. Within it, one blue rose grew, and behind it stood a rune-stone.

"There's the rose," said Brunhilde. Her teeth chattered. "That stone must go to the ice mountains of Niflheim, but we have to turn it on. You want to give it a shot, Thundercluck?"

The chicken pointed his wings and closed his eyes. In his mind he heard the Cook's laughter, and no thunder would come.

"It's okay," Brunhilde said.

Thundercluck gave a weak nod.

The girl held his gaze and said, "I'm glad you're with me. I wouldn't want to do this alone."

He felt warmth in his chest and thought, *I don't know what's wrong with my powers . . . but I can help my friend.*

Brunhilde slashed with her glowing sword.

CLANG!

The runes glowed blue, and the heroes stepped on the platform. In a flash of cool light, they vanished.

While Alfheim had been warm and pleasant, Niflheim was the polar opposite. The heroes braced themselves against heavy snow. Jagged mountains surrounded them. Brunhilde had packed a pair of scarves, but when she put one on Thundercluck, he still felt cold.

At least I look fancy, he thought.

Brunhilde shivered and said, "Niflheim . . . More like Sniffle-heim, am I right?"

Silence followed, save for the whistling wind. In the distance they heard a sound: "Baa-a-a."

Brunhilde opened the book again and said, "Niflheim." The pages fluttered to a poem and stayed there, even though the wind was fierce. The poem read:

THROUGH NIFLHEIM (A LIMERICK)

There once were some kids on a cliff.
They climbed a rock over a rift.
It wasn't humongous,
But there they found fungus,
And shelter from flurries adrift.

"Okay," Brunhilde said, "so we're looking for . . . kids? Other than ourselves?" They looked around. Aside from the snow in the wind, nothing moved.

In the distance they heard another "Baa-a-a." Thundercluck tilted his head and cocked an eyebrow at Brunhilde.

They flew toward the sound and discovered two young mountain goats on a cliff.

"Oh," Brunhilde said. "They're kids . . . as in goats."

They stood above a deep crevice. A mountain towered over them, rising into clouds so thick they blocked the summit from sight.

"I think we're supposed to go up there," Brunhilde said, "but I don't know if we can climb the rock, and I don't think we should fly in those clouds. How do we get up?"

"Baa-a-a," said one of the goats, and it started climbing the cliff. Where the heroes would be sure to slip, the mountain goat seemed perfectly secure.

"Hey, wait," Brunhilde said. "Can we catch a ride?"

The goat stared at her blankly.

"I'll take that as a yes." She and Thundercluck each jumped on a goat, and they climbed into the mist.

On goat-back they rode to the top of the clouds, and still the mountain rose higher. The air became clear, and the heroes could fly. They tried to thank the goats with snacks, but the goats seemed more interested in trying to eat their backpacks.

Brunhilde gave her goat a half pat, half push away, and the heroes took flight. They landed on top of the mountain.

"Well, I'm exhausted," Brunhilde said. "Who knew staying on a goat would take so much effort?"

Thundercluck nodded with sleepy eyes.

They made camp and slept, then woke at dawn. A star twinkled out, leaving seven in the sky.

These are dark times, Thundercluck thought. He solemnly whispered, "Bagaw."

Then a spot in the snow caught his eye. He pecked at it and pulled up a mushroom.

"The poem said, 'There they found fungus,'" Brunhilde said. "We must be close to our next goal!"

They followed a trail of mushrooms down the far side of the rocky spire. It led to a cave, which held more mushrooms and a rune-stone.

Thundercluck looked at the stone, then at his wings. He lowered his head. Brunhilde patted his neck feathers and cast her own light on the stone.

CLANG!

The runes glowed with copper light.

"Because of the mushrooms," Brunhilde said, "I'm guessing this goes to Vanaheim, the realm of woods and rivers. Shall we?"

They stepped onto the platform, and copper light carried them to their next stop.

When the light faded, the heroes found themselves in a forest. After the darkness of Niflheim, Thundercluck had to shield his eyes from the morning sun.

Trees towered overhead, and mushrooms covered the ground. A river flowed nearby, and a turtle bobbed on its surface.

Brunhilde opened the book and said, "Vanaheim." It flipped to a page that read:

THROUGH VANAHEIM (AN ACROSTIC RHYME)

To reach the sea,
Unfurl the sail.
Rely upon the ship.
To pass the beast,
Look out—the tail!
Engage its fragile tip.

Brunhilde looked around. "So . . . do you see a ship or a sail anywhere?"

Thundercluck went to the river. He glanced upstream and down, but he saw no boat.

They read the poem again. "If there's a sea," Brunhilde said, "we could probably find it by flying, but it sounds like we're supposed to use a boat." She sighed. "Good gods, author, just draw a map!"

She started to close the book, but something caught Thundercluck's eye. He stuck his wing on the page and traced the first letter of each line.

His eyes widened.

He turned to the river, where the turtle still bobbed. Flying closer, he saw that it was wooden, and he landed on its shell. It started to rise.

A boat emerged from the river with a splash. The turtle was an ornament on its prow.

"You found it!" Brunhilde said. She flew to the boat and unfurled its sail. By some magic, it was dry.

"This is Asgardian," she said. "I learned in history class that our people came here years ago."

The boat had a steering wheel, but it set itself into motion. It drifted on the river of Vanaheim, passing under branches and moss. Thundercluck leaned overboard and stared at his reflection.

I'm helping with the riddles, he thought, *but I wish I had my thunder. If we meet a monster, I'm useless.*

Brunhilde smiled his way, and then motion on the shore caught her attention. Slender robed figures were watching them from the trees.

"Those are the Vanir," Brunhilde said, waving, "the native people of this realm. Years ago there was a war between the Vanir and the Asgardians."

Thundercluck raised his brows and looked at their tranquil surroundings.

"It's settled now," Brunhilde said. "Odin made a truce with Vanaheim before I was born, and now Asgardians and Vanir live together in peace."

A young Vanir waved at Thundercluck. Slowly, the chicken waved back.

Brunhilde continued. "No one's ever told me why the war started. They just say, 'It's complicated.' But I think part of it was fear. Both sides were afraid of what they didn't understand."

The boat passed through a delta and emerged at sea. The mossy trees gave way to clear sky, and seagulls hovered above.

Brunhilde stared at the ocean and said, "Sometimes fear makes us act weird, and we regret it later. But we can learn from it." She put her hand on the chicken's shoulder. "What I'm trying to say is ... Wait. Something's not right."

The seagulls had flown away, and the water had gone still. The sudden quiet made Thundercluck's neck feathers stand on end.

BLUB-BLUB-BLUB!

A ring of sharp rocks bubbled up from the sea, encircling the boat and snaring the heroes in a watery trap. The roiling water calmed, but a shadow moved under its surface.

SPLASH!

A massive, scaly sea monster burst from the depths. It towered over the boat. Its eyes bulged, and rows of teeth glistened in its mouth.

"It's a Collosa-Carp!" Brunhilde shouted. "It wants

to smash us! We can't fly away—dry land is too far. We've got to get the boat free!" She grabbed the steering wheel and scanned the rocks. "There's a gap I can fit us through. I can steer . . . but, Thundercluck, I need you to hold off the monster!"

The chicken gulped.

The monster surged, causing a wave to rush at the boat. Brunhilde yelled, "There's no way I can dodge that wave—it'll push us into the rocks!"

I don't have my thunder, the chicken thought, *but I still have my wings!* He jumped and flapped hard, blowing a gust of wind at the sail. The boat lifted over the wave. Water crashed on the rocks around them, but the boat was safe.

"Nice work!" Brunhilde called.

The monster looked furious and raised its tail high to crush the boat. Most of the tail was covered in thick scales, but the scales at its tip were thinner. *Engage its fragile tip,* Thundercluck remembered from the poem.

The tail rose higher. Thundercluck flew after it. He grabbed the tail with his feet, stretched his head back, and jabbed at the tip like a woodpecker.

The creature jerked back and roared, and Thundercluck fluttered away. The Collosa-Carp put its tail in its mouth, groaned, and sank beneath the sea. The groan became bubbles. Then all was still.

Brunhilde steered between the rocks, and Thundercluck landed beside her.

"Thanks, buddy—you did it!" she said. "Let's see where the ship takes us."

After hours at sea, Thundercluck stared at the sunset. *I did something good*, he thought. *I saved my friend. But still . . .* He looked at his wings.

"Hey," Brunhilde said, stepping away from the steering wheel. "The boat's steering itself, so let's get some rest."

She gave him a squeeze and added, "Thanks again, warrior bird."

BONK.

The heroes awoke to a thump. The boat had come ashore on a beach where a rune-stone sat under a coconut tree. Brunhilde tied the boat to the tree, and the heroes studied the stone. Glowing coals surrounded it.

Brunhilde sniffed the coals and said, "This must go to Muspellheim." She turned to Thundercluck and asked, "Still no bolts?"

Thundercluck shook his head.

"Don't worry," Brunhilde said. "But listen. This next one's the realm of fire, and I know that might be scary for you. I'm proud of you, and I know you can be brave."

Thundercluck nodded, and he tried not to dwell on the dangers ahead.

The sun began to rise, and a third star twinkled out. Six more remained.

Brunhilde cast light upon the stone, and it sounded with a familiar CLANG!

The runes glowed red, lighting the heroes like a fire. "To Muspellheim!" Brunhilde said, and together they leapt into the light.

CHAPTER 13
INTO THE FIRE

THE HEROES ARRIVED ON DARK ROCKS
beneath a fiery sky. The air smelled like smoke. There
were craggy mountains in all directions, and a distant
volcano smoldered.

Brunhilde looked in the book and said, "Muspellheim." It opened to a poem:

THROUGH MUSPELLHEIM (A VALKAMOR VERSE)

The one with the scales looks over the trail.
A choice at the end you'll discover.
One stone for the tree . . . and danger, you see.
To safety on Earth goes the other.

Thundercluck's eyes went wide. *To safety on Earth?* he thought. *A way back to the farm?*

Brunhilde glanced around and said, "Hey, look, this one's easy." She pointed to a rock shaped like a lizard and a path right beside it. "Lizards have scales, and there's a trail. We just follow that, and bam, we get to the tree."

Thundercluck had trouble moving. He knew going to the tree was right, but in his head he imagined the farm.

"Remember that dragon, Blimpor?" Brunhilde said. "This is his home realm, and it's the land of the man-pigs, too. We'll have to go on foot. If we fly, they might see us."

Thundercluck nodded. At least the path went away from the volcano.

"It might be a long hike," Brunhilde said, "so let's get started."

After hiking all day, they made camp. Brunhilde went into her tent, but Thundercluck stayed out alone.

A river of lava flowed alongside the trail. Thunder-cluck sat by it and felt its glow on his feathers. He daydreamed about having his power back, defeating the Cook with a bolt, and returning home a hero. *If only it were that easy,* he thought. *What happened to my thunder?*

"You're wondering if you're cursed," Brunhilde said, emerging from her tent. She sat down. "I don't think that's it, though." She tapped him on the head and said, "I think your problem is here."

"Buk . . . buk-bwak?" Thun-dercluck said, his voice soft and shaky.

"It was scary when Gorman attacked us," Brunhilde went on. "You panicked, and you couldn't help when Thor was taken. Since then, you haven't had your thunder."

The chicken felt like hiding in his tent, but he knew he should stay and listen. It helped that Brunhilde's smile was kind.

"I know what it's like," she said. "And I know you can learn from it."

Thundercluck cocked his head. Brunhilde adjusted her helmet.

"When I got this helmet, it meant I was ready for missions, and that's when Odin put me on patrol. Usually it was busywork: take a little walk, write a little report. But one day was different."

A distant look came into her eyes. Thundercluck leaned toward her.

"I found a group of man-pigs trying to break through one of our walls with a giant, armored boar. They called him Big Borris, the Wall Buster."

The chicken blinked.

"I tried to hit him with my magic," she said. "I'd trained so hard and passed all my tests. I thought I was unstoppable. But his armor was enchanted, and my attack bounced away like it was nothing."

Thundercluck remembered that *uh-oh* feeling from the wolf and the dragon.

"I just froze," Brunhilde said, "and Borris charged at

me. Then I heard thunder, and Borris stopped. He was so close, I felt his stinky breath on my face. We both looked up, and Thor was on the wall. He'd summoned a storm."

She smiled at Thundercluck.

"Big Borris turned and ran, and all the man-pigs followed. Apparently Borris was scared of thunder . . . I guess everyone's scared of something." She looked off at the volcano. "I was so ashamed," she whispered. "The next day I kept thinking, *Maybe yesterday* . . .

Maybe if I'd had different magic; maybe if I'd had a different sword . . ."

She drew her weapon. "By the way," she said, "the only sword finer than Asgardian crystal"—she turned her hilt in the lava light—"is a Dwarven Blade. Dwarves make *the best* swords. But they're rare . . . and the sword wasn't what really mattered."

She put her blade back in its sheath. "What really mattered," she said, "was me. I had panicked, and I knew I could do better. So I stopped thinking, *Maybe*

yesterday, and I started thinking, *Maybe today. Maybe today, I can be brave.*"

Thundercluck leaned his head on Brunhilde's shoulder. *You've always been brave to me,* he thought. *I thought you weren't scared of anything!*

She ruffled his feathers and said, "I still wish I hadn't frozen that day, but I learned from it. Deep down, there's a bit of fear in every adventure." She smiled. "Sometimes a *lot* of fear. All we can do is accept that it's scary and give it our best shot anyway."

Night was coming, and the red sky was getting dark.

"Thor saved me that day," she said, "and maybe I can return the favor . . . especially with *you* on my side." She winked, then got up and went to her tent. She turned and said, "Good night, warrior bird. You know I believe in you."

Thundercluck stared at the volcano, and he tried to believe, too.

They spent four days hiking through Muspellheim. Each night, Thundercluck struggled to sleep. Each morning, another star faded.

By the fifth sunrise in the realm, only two stars remained.

"We're running out of time," Brunhilde said, "but I think we're close."

That afternoon the heroes reached a corner on a narrow ledge. On one side was a rock wall, and on the other, a sheer drop to lava. The air was hot, and the heroes were tired. Brunhilde called for a pause.

"Wait . . ." Brunhilde said. "Do you hear that?"

They both listened. Around the corner came squeals and snorts.

"Man-pigs!" Brunhilde whispered. "We can't make a sound!"

Alarmed, Thundercluck jumped back and hit a rock. It rolled toward the edge and fell into the lava with a splash. The chicken squawked and fluttered his wings in fright.

"Whuzzat noise?"

"I mighta heard wings!"

"We gotta check. If it's that chicken, we're gonna make Boss Bones real happy!"

Thundercluck buried his face in his wing as Brunhilde grabbed her sword. The man-pigs were coming.

CHAPTER 14
THE BREAKING POINT

SILENTLY, BRUNHILDE NUDGED THUNDER-cluck and looked up the rock wall. The heroes nodded and flew upward together. The top of the cliff was flat, and upon it was a boulder with a crack at its base. The heroes pressed against it. They heard the man-pigs below.

"No one's here!"

"But look, feathers!"

"Whoever it was, I bet they flew up. Let's climb!"

Thundercluck almost squawked again, but Brunhilde covered his beak. She whispered, "They don't know there's two of us! I don't want you fighting without your thunder, so you hide in the boulder, and I'll handle the pigs."

They heard the man-pigs climbing, and Thundercluck scurried into the boulder's crack. Brunhilde wedged her shield in front of him. Thundercluck could see out, but no one could see in.

The hogs clambered into view. From his hiding spot, Thundercluck counted three of them.

"Hey," one shouted at Brunhilde. "You're not a chicken, you're a girl!"

"Aren't *you* observant?" Brunhilde said, and her helmet dropped into battle mode.

"Boss Bones didn't say nuthin' 'bout a girl," another pig snorted, "but let's take her hostage. Maybe she can serve us in the dining hall!"

Brunhilde twirled her sword. "Oh, you're getting served, all right."

The man-pigs charged, but the warrior girl was ready. She dodged and kicked two of them together, then sent the third flying with an arc of light.

Thundercluck wiggled and thought, *Way to go, Brunhilde! We'll be out of here in no time.*

The flying pig hit the ground with a thud. "This was a mistake," he moaned. "Call Captain War-Tog!"

One of the others lifted a horn from his belt and blew on it. A low note rang through the air.

Sounds of a pickax and grunting quickly followed, and a bigger man-pig heaved himself onto the cliff. Brunhilde recognized him from Valhalla.

War-Tog gaped. "That's Brunhilde!"

One of the fallen pigs wheezed, "Who?"

War-Tog snorted. "When Boss Bones went to As-gard, me and three pigs tried to fight her. But she whupped us! We gotta call Boss!"

The other man-pigs staggered back. War-Tog struck a wide stance, took a deep breath, and raised a tiny dinner bell. He rang it in the air.

A cloud of smoke swept over the cliff. It swirled in a vortex. When it parted, there stood Gorman Bones.

Thundercluck trembled. *Brunhilde might need me to help*, he thought, *but I can't! I was so scared last time . . . and back then I still had my thunder!*

"Well," said the chef, his voice like smoking char-coal, "what do we have here? You've made yourself useful, War-Tog—for once! I suppose even a blind pig can sniff out a truffle."

War-Tog pretended he understood what that meant. He nodded quietly.

Brunhilde glared at the Cook. Her eyes were hidden beneath her helmet, but still the chef could feel their contempt.

"I have questions for you, girl," he said.

"Well, I don't feel like talking!" Brunhilde said. She slashed her sword's magic at the Cook.

He held up his frying pan to intercept it, and the magic bounced away. Brunhilde frowned. The chef grinned from the pan to the girl. "Nonstick coating, you see."

Brunhilde's deflected light flew off into the distance, but then . . .

CLANG!

I know that sound, Thundercluck thought. *That was a rune-stone! Maybe we can escape!* He tried to move, but it felt like his feet were stuck to the ground. He was a frozen chicken yet again.

Gorman kept grinning at Brunhilde. "You've been a thorn in my side, girl . . . Now, let me teach you some respect!"

With a whoosh of smoke, he darted forward and swung down his pan. Brunhilde's sword glowed brighter than ever before, and she swung it up at the chef. The weapons collided with a flash of light and the sound of shattering glass.

Thundercluck covered his eyes, then slowly peered out from behind the shield. His giblets quivered.

Brunhilde, still standing, was holding the hilt of her

sword. It vibrated with a dying hum. Shards of crystal were sprinkled all around her. The Valkyrie's blade had broken.

Fury shone in her eyes.

"Now," said the chef, "you've lost your sword, and I don't see your shield . . . perhaps you'll talk, after all."

But War-Tog spoke first. "How'd you do it, Boss? Last time you two fought, her sword could stop your pan!"

"Oh, just a bit of kitchen magic," the Cook replied. He whirled his pan in the air, sending up pillars of flame. Then he held the pan close, eyeing the notch Brunhilde had cut in it before. "After Asgard," he said, "I knew this pan needed more enchantment. So first I fried some dragon scales—medium heat, mind you— then I deglazed the pan with the grease of an elbow, and the blood from a stone, and then—"

"I don't care," Brunhilde said, dropping her bladeless hilt to the ground. "Do you ever *not* talk about cooking?"

"Hmph," Gorman said. "I spend hours in the kitchen, and no one appreciates it. Now, tell me . . . where is the chicken?"

"No idea," Brunhilde said. "He and I split up a while back . . . He had a lead on how to bring you down. I bet by now he knows your weakness!"

Thundercluck squirmed in his hiding place.

One of the pigs grunted and said, "But I heard wings, and we saw feathers. I thought it was the chicken!"

Brunhilde said, "Those were mine, genius," and she gave her wings a flutter. "You know I have these, right?"

The Cook glared at the girl and said, "Very well. I'm preparing a dinner party, and I insist that you be my guest." He nodded at War-Tog, who lumbered over to Brunhilde. The pig picked up her fallen hilt and chained her wrists together.

"Perhaps . . ." the chef continued, gazing around the plateau, "with a bit of luck, Thundercluck might join us."

He tossed a handful of spices into his pan, and a cloud of smoke erupted. It engulfed the Cook, the girl, and the pigs ... and then it blew away. Everyone was gone.

Thundercluck was alone.

CHAPTER 15
THE CHICKEN'S CHOICE

THUNDERCLUCK PEEKED OUT FROM inside the boulder. The cliff was deserted, as was the path below. He wriggled through the crack, and the shield popped out with him. He grabbed it with his foot and secured it to his backpack. He looked around, lonesome and desolate, and wondered what to do.

The more he thought, the more fear took over. *I'm alone! Brunhilde knew what to do, but she's gone! What do I do?*

His heart was racing, and he waddled in circles, clucking as he went.

"Buk-buk-buk-buk-buk..."

He made himself dizzy, then took a deep breath and tried to calm down.

Okay, he thought. *Earlier, I heard a CLANG—that was a rune-stone turning on. The book said there were two, one for the tree, the other for Earth. I'll just follow the path and find the stones!*

The chicken flew low, and soon he arrived at a flat sheet of rock. On its surface, two rune-stones waited side by side. One was dark, and the other glowed with magic.

Thundercluck landed and looked from one stone to the other. Both had moss around their bases, but they smelled different. The dim, unlit stone had an otherworldly smell that filled Thundercluck with wonder. The glowing stone smelled like the farm.

The only stone ready to use, thought Thundercluck, *is the one that takes me back to safety!*

He looked from stone to stone. Holding his wings to his chest, he felt no power inside himself.

I guess that's it, he thought. *If I had my thunder, I could activate the other stone and get to the cosmic tree . . . But I don't have it. I've done all I can. And Brunhilde wanted me to be safe. So I should go back to the farm.*

He nodded to himself and thought, *Well, I tried. I've had a good run, but I'm going back to the farm. Maybe this time, I'll pretend I fit in.*

When he tried to step on the platform, though, his feet refused to move.

The chicken thought, *Huh? That happens when the Cook's around, but he's nowhere near! Why am I afraid? I'll finally be safe!*

He looked back at the other stone. Then he thought about his quest, Thor, and Brunhilde—and found his feet could move again.

At the other end of Muspellheim, Gorman Bones and War-Tog led Brunhilde in chains. They marched to the giant volcano. Its base was surrounded by a lava moat. A drawbridge lowered before them, and a pair of towering gates flew open.

"Welcome," said the Cook, "to Castle Igneous."

Brunhilde frowned. She sniffed the air. "Smells like something's burning."

"When I'm done cooking," the chef replied, "*everything* will burn." He turned to War-Tog. "You!

Take our guest to her cage. I'll check on Thor, and then I'll be up to visit." He vanished in a puff of smoke.

So Thor's alive, Brunhilde thought. She wiggled her wrists, but the chains held tight. *I need to escape, but first I should scope this place out.*

She followed War-Tog through the gates and into a passageway. The gates slammed shut, and torches lit themselves along the passage.

Brunhilde whistled. "Quite a collection!"

Sculptures, paintings, and tapestries lined the tunnel. Every single piece of art had some kind of chicken in it.

She elbowed War-Tog. "He's like an art collector, except he's insane."

War-Tog shrugged. "Some people are both. 'Specially Boss." He bumped into a sculpture of a dancing rooster. "I just follow orders. Boss wants a chicken art? We bring him a chicken art." He glanced from side to side, and whispered, "Mr. Boss has specific tastes."

War-Tog led Brunhilde through the tunnel, which took them to a cavernous dining hall. Tables, chairs, and dirty dishes filled the room.

"This is where he feeds us," War-Tog said. "Boss calls it, uh, the Dining Hall of Doom. We used to be *regular* pigs, but Boss . . . Boss gave us gruel." He burped, then added, "We got big and smart."

Well, I can agree with "big," Brunhilde thought. She nodded.

"This volcano's full of caves," the pig went on, "and Boss made it his castle. Over there, that's where he cooks. With the lava."

War-Tog pointed to a pair of doors across the room.

One door was high on a balcony, and the other was at ground level.

"That top door," War-Tog said, "Boss calls that the Kitchen of Destiny. The lower one, that's the Pantry of Peril. That's where he keeps all his stuff."

War-Tog led Brunhilde to a smaller side door. It creaked open, and they left the Dining Hall of Doom.

They trudged through a twisting cave. Brunhilde's chains rattled, and the sound echoed ahead. When they reached a side cave, War-Tog said, "Here's your room."

Inside was a human-sized birdcage suspended over a lava pool.

War-Tog took Brunhilde's Battle Bag. "I keep this," he said. "Boss says you gotta get in the cage." She sighed and hopped in. War-Tog locked the cage and took the chains off her wrists.

A cloud of smoke appeared, and Gorman Bones emerged.

War-Tog saluted. "Welcome, Boss!"

The Cook ignored the pig and leaned over the lava toward Brunhilde. "How do you like the view?" he asked.

"I can take it or leave it," Brunhilde replied, "but I can't stand the company."

"Well," Gorman said with a grin, "too bad, young lady, because we have more to discuss. You saw Thor strike me down all those years ago. Tell me, don't you wonder how I survived?"

Brunhilde's eyes narrowed. "I've got a big list of priorities," she said, "and that question's down at the bot—"

"You see," the Cook interrupted, "when Thor's bolt hit me, it zapped me into Helheim, the realm of the dead. It was a land of fossil and shadow. I had become a skeleton, stripped of my flesh and blood!"

War-Tog's mouth gaped. Brunhilde crossed her arms and thought, *Here we go.*

"I journeyed across mountains of ash and valleys of bone," the chef went on, "and at last I reached the palace, Eljudnir! There lives Hel, the Goddess of Death.

Once a soul enters her realm, she *never* lets it out—but we made a deal. For I knew Helheim had the darkest cocoa powder in all the realms. So in return for my freedom, I promised Hel . . . the greatest fudge brownie any world has ever witnessed."

War-Tog gasped. "What was innit, Boss?"

"Oh, a little of this, a little of that. The legs of a fish, the beard of a bat. And I offered pecans, but the Goddess has a nut allergy." His eyes took on a distant look. "I toiled in Hel's kitchen for days, months, years! And when it was done . . . *the brownie was spectacular.* The Goddess of Death was pleased, and I was freed. So you see"—he ended with dramatic flourish—"I cheated death by chocolate."

War-Tog squealed and applauded. Brunhilde groaned.

"I returned to the realms of the living," Gorman said, "and then I plotted my revenge. I learned to teleport with my smoke. I enchanted my cookware for battle!" He lifted his pan with pride.

War-Tog nodded and said, "Tell her 'bout the army, Boss!"

"Yes," answered Gorman. "Yes, it was all me! My food brought the monsters together! My food made them stronger! I've been commanding the man-pigs. It was me all along!"

"You don't say," Brunhilde replied, still giving him a flat look.

"I see you're not impressed," said the chef. "What, do you think the chicken will come? Oh, I bet he will...and when he does, I'll be ready."

Brunhilde's face held firm, but her heart skipped

a beat. She clutched the locket Saga had given her.

"You see," the Cook went on, "I have quite the appetite for that bird." He held up a hand and stared at the bones of his fingers. "My skeleton arose from the underworld, but my flesh was lost. Once I eat that chicken, though, I'll absorb his power—and I'll have my body back!" He looked Brunhilde up and down, and added, "A high-protein diet does wonders for the figure, dear."

Brunhilde's eyes rolled so far, she thought she could see her brain.

"And that's not all!" the Cook declared. From his apron he withdrew *The Recipe Book of the Dead*. "Let's see here," he muttered, flipping through its tattered pages, "there's Beastly Barbecue, Nefarious Fondue . . . Ah yes, here it is." He turned the book to Brunhilde, who read the grim recipe: Chicken Soup for the Wretched Soul.

"When little Thundercluck comes to face my army," Gorman whispered, "we'll have ourselves a stew."

There was a moment of silence, then Brunhilde asked, "Aren't soup and stew technically different—"

"Irrelevant!" barked the chef. He straightened his cook's hat, and his mustache curled upward with his smile. "When the chicken arrives, I will cook him in my cauldron. All the meat will be mine, but my man-pigs will feast on his broth. Then I'll have my body back, and my army will be unstoppable!"

Brunhilde frowned, and her eyes widened.

"And here's the best part," Gorman said, enunciating every word. "When I eat Thundercluck, you and Thor ... are going to watch. Yes, yes! I'll chain you both in the dining hall, and once the soup is on, I'll wake Thor back up. And then I'll have my feast!"

Gorman chuckled as he turned to leave the room. He paused at the doorway and looked over his shoulder to add, "See you at the dinner party!"

He threw back his skull with a cackle and strode from the chamber. He was gone, but his laughter echoed behind him.

War-Tog smirked at Brunhilde, then turned to follow the Cook.

"Wait," she said, and the man-pig stopped. Brunhilde gripped her cage, staring at her bag draped on War-Tog's shoulder. "You have my Battle Ba ... Ahem, you have my *purse*," she said.

War-Tog stiffened. "So what?" he asked. "Wha's innit?"

"Lots of stuff," Brunhilde said, "but all I want is my nail file." She held up her hands. "I always forget about my nails when I travel ... but if I'm going to a dinner party, I ought to look nice."

War-Tog's glare was half suspicious, half confused.

Brunhilde shrugged and said, "I think it's what Gor—It's what *Mr. Boss* would want." She looked at the pig's nails. They were crusty and of various lengths. "If you stick around, can I do yours, too?"

"No!" War-Tog grunted. "No, you, uh ... You wanna look nice, all yours." He picked out the nail file and tossed it to her.

Brunhilde smiled sweetly.

The pig left, and Brunhilde's smile dropped. The file was made of Asgardian gold, the toughest metal in all the realms. She took a deep breath and started filing through one of the cage's bars.

Thundercluck stared at the darkened stone. Memories flooded his mind.

He thought about his childhood, when he had always wanted to explore. He thought about his mom, the only chicken who had been nice to him. He thought about Asgard, the one place that felt like home. He thought about Thor, the closest thing he had to a father.

And most of all, Thundercluck thought about Brunhilde. She had believed in him every step of the way, and she had given herself up to keep him safe.

He felt a charge of thunder rising in his chest. His eyes glowed with determination. He gripped the ground with his feet and pointed his wings at the darkened stone.

For a moment, all was quiet.

This is for my friends, the chicken thought. Then he unleashed a "Buk, ba-GAACK!"

A thunderbolt flowed through his chest and erupted from his wings. It struck the stone with a *CLANG!* The stone glowed with purple light. Its platform was ready to go.

Thundercluck looked at his wings, then turned his gaze to the stone.

Onward, he thought.

Back in Valhalla, the Asgardians were still asleep... but one goddess stirred.

Saga twisted and turned. Her eyes remained shut, but in her sleep she murmured:

> *Our heroes are divided now . . .*
> *The pair is torn asunder . . .*

Yet Thundercluck has powered on . . .

The chicken found his thunder!

The maiden has the will to fight . . .

The bird is standing tall . . .

It's up to them to reunite . . . and then to save us all!

PART IV

THUNDERCLUCK
RETURNS

CHAPTER 16
THE ROOTS

THUNDERCLUCK ARRIVED ON AN ISLAND of moss and crystals. Beyond the shoreline, perfectly still water spread in all directions. The island held a massive tree, wider than the Castle of Asgard and taller than the eye could see. Even the tree's roots were taller than Thundercluck's head.

Countless stars shone above. The brightest were the two that remained for Asgard's magic.

So this is Yggdrasil, the chicken thought. *It truly is majestic.*

"Bagurrrrrrk," he said out loud.

A stone well sat among the roots. Thundercluck started toward it, then paused. At first the silence had felt calm. Now it felt eerie.

I can't give up, he thought. *I've got my powers back, and my friends are counting on me!*

He thought he saw movement from the corner of his eye. He jerked his head to look, but all was still. He saw his reflection in a crystal, and then noticed something moving behind him. He whipped around, but again there was nothing to see.

He was a few paces from the well when he heard the slithering.

A tree root, thicker than the others, was

moving. It curled in front of Thundercluck, and its end arched over the well like a giant finger pointing at the bird.

Thundercluck stared at the root's tip in confusion. Suddenly, two eyes flashed open, and the tip stared back. This was no tree root—it was a massive snake!

The serpent shed its magic disguise, and its scales turned violet. It reared over the well and flicked its tongue. The snake was big enough to swallow the chicken whole.

Thundercluck gulped. *Is this the elder that the book said to find?*

"Greetingssss, chicken," the snake hissed. "I am

Nidhogg, ssserpent of the tree. If it's knowledge you ssseek, you must prove yourself worthy, for these roots are my home...and you look like my dinner!"

The serpent lunged at Thundercluck. Its mouth opened wide, showing fangs and a cavernous throat. The chicken dodged and thought, *Good thing I've got my thunder back. Time to put it to use!*

KRA-KOWWW!

He launched a crackling bolt, striking the snake on its neck.

The serpent flinched as arcs of lightning sizzled up and down its body. "Sssso," it said, "you're a *magic* chicken! That meanss you'll be all the more scrumptioussss!"

Those scales are magic-proof, thought Thundercluck. *I've counted on Brunhilde to help me find weak points . . . but I have to do this alone.*

The serpent closed its eyes, and its skin looked like a root again. Thundercluck's heart beat faster. Suddenly roots were moving all around him! He had no idea where the head was, or when the next bite was coming.

Don't panic, he thought. *If I can't see the head, I'll use my other senses.* He closed his eyes and heard a hiss. *That's it!*

The serpent lashed toward him, and Thundercluck spun out of the way just in time. With his eyes shut tight, the chicken blasted another bolt, aiming at where he had heard the sound.

The snake hissed again, this time in fury. Thundercluck opened an eye to peek. The lightning had struck its face. The serpent shuddered, and its scales flashed in waves of color. Then they settled, and once more the snake looked like a root. Thundercluck closed his eyes and listened again.

"Very clever," the serpent said. "You have good ears . . . but they won't hear thiss coming!"

THWACK!

Something hit Thundercluck, sending him flying into the air. The snake had smacked him with its tail.

CHOMP!

Thundercluck opened his eyes, but everything was dark. He felt slimy pressure pushing at him from every direction. Horrified, he realized where he was.

He was in the serpent's mouth. Nidhogg had caught him.

Thundercluck tried to squirm, but he could hardly move. The mouth seemed to slide around him. He was being swallowed.

This is it. This is how it ends. Fear coursed through him, but part of his mind thought, *It's almost funny—I was so afraid of the Under-Cook, but then some other monster got me.*

Then he thought, *No . . . This is NOT how it ends. I'm not done with that Cook!*

Defiance swirled in his chest, and he felt a surge of

thunder unlike any before. It flowed to the tips of all the feathers on his body.

I am Thundercluck of Asgard, he thought, *and I shall prevail!*

"Ba-GURRRK!" he cried out. Lightning erupted from him in all directions.

The serpent spasmed and shook, unprepared for a shock from the inside. It tried to keep its mouth shut, but the thunder was too much. The snake spat out the chicken.

When he pried open his spit-soaked eyelids, Thundercluck saw the serpent slithering back toward the tree's roots.

"You have proved yourself worthy," Nidhogg said, "and ssspicy, too." As the snake vanished through a hole in the roots, its voice echoed. "I'll eat something elssse."

All was calm.

So . . . that probably wasn't the elder, the chicken thought. *Maybe the elder meets people by that stone well.*

He straightened his helmet and walked to the well,

but he saw no one. The island, the tree, and the water: everything was perfectly still.

He peered into the well and thought, *What now?* Thundercluck looked at himself in the water below. Then his eyebrows shot up. In the reflection, he saw a woman standing beside him.

"Well met, Thunder- cluck," said the woman. "I am Urd, the Keeper of Fates, and this is the Well of Eternity."

CHAPTER 17

THE WELL OF ETERNITY

THUNDERCLUCK JUMPED AND SPUN around, but no one was there. He looked in the well, and in the water he saw Urd once more. In the pool's reflection, it looked like she was standing right by his shoulder.

"Few will ever see me," she said, "for they know not where to look." She gazed at the cosmic tree. "Outside this well, I am unseen ... but from within, I have seen for ages."

Her face was ancient and beautiful. Deep wrinkles flowed from her eyes to her temples. They possessed an elegance, as if they held the stories of time itself.

"You see my age, chicken," Urd said, "and you see the tales I know. Do you see, though, how you yourself have grown?"

Thundercluck looked at his own reflection. He thought about his journey, recalling his thunder's fade and return. *It's not just that I have my power again,* he thought. *I feel different.*

Urd read his eyes and said, "Your journey, warrior bird, is not yet complete." In the reflection, she put her hand on his shoulder. Thundercluck felt it.

"Each time you saw the chef," she went on, "you feared for your own safety. But when you almost gave up, you came to fear for others. You care about your friends as much as yourself. When you realized this . . . *that* was when your thunder returned."

The chicken thought about his mother, and about the Asgardians, all trapped by the cursed pie. He thought about Thor and Brunhilde, both taken by the Cook. His wattles shook.

Urd held his gaze and said, "You chose not to run, and know this: you chose well. Had you given up, the Under-Cook would have scoured the realms to find you."

Thundercluck remembered Sven and Olga. *They gave me shelter,* he thought, *and I almost brought them doom.*

He looked up at the tree. Its trunk seemed to climb to infinity. The bird imagined its branches, beyond what the eye could see. He knew they cradled the realms.

"If you fail to stop Gorman Bones," Urd said, "no world will escape his wrath."

Thundercluck blinked at the well. *How do I find him?*

From the pool, Urd's gaze returned to the chicken. "The Cook is waiting for you," she said. "He has the power to travel between realms, but for now he has exhausted that magic. He waits in the fires of Muspellheim, where he expects you to meet him."

The chicken gulped.

"You must face him soon," the teller continued, "but not yet."

She waved her hands, and Yggdrasil's roots began to move.

Unlike the serpent, whose writhing had seemed vile and sinister, the true roots flowed with grace. They spiraled together into a nest, and Thundercluck realized his eyelids were heavy.

"Voyage and battle have left you weary," Urd said. "Now, you must rest."

How long has it been, Thundercluck wondered, *since I've slept without a nightmare?* He looked into the well with gratitude in his eyes. Urd nodded.

Thundercluck fell fast asleep, and Urd gazed at the two remaining Aurora stars. "Hold fast, Asgardians," she said. "When he awakens...I will prepare the chicken."

Back in Castle Igneous, Brunhilde huffed and puffed as she filed at the bar. The cage swung from side to side, and iron dust fell into the lava.

Brunhilde paused and looked at the chamber's door. *As soon as I break through this bar,* she thought, *I'll bust out and whup some pigs!* Then worry crept into her mind. *My sword is broken, my shield is gone, I don't know where Thor is . . . and I don't know if Thundercluck is okay!*

She took a deep breath and exhaled. "One thing at a time," she said. "Focus on what can be done now." She went back to filing the cage.

It seemed like ages before, finally, the file passed

through, and Brunhilde grabbed the bar. With its top detached, it wiggled, but its base was still fixed to the cage.

She panted and wiped her brow. Her muscles ached. Blisters rose on her fingers. *Well*, she thought, *that's the halfway point. Top is done . . . Time to start the bottom.*

Elsewhere in the castle, man-pigs licked their lips. They were hungry for power. They were hungry for battle. They were hungry for chicken.

The dinner party drew near.

Thundercluck slept on Yggdrasil's roots, and the cosmic sky shimmered above. The chicken dreamed again of the Cook. Instead of a terrible chase, though, this time the dream was a battle. The bird and the chef collided, attacking each other with lightning and fire. Thundercluck had never felt stronger, but the villain seemed invincible. As the battle raged on, the chicken's hope dwindled.

Thundercluck opened his eyes. *I have my thunder back,*

he thought, *but what if it's not enough?* He closed his eyes, but sleep would not return.

"Arise, chicken," Urd's voice called. Thundercluck stood and shook his feathers. He went to the well.

Urd's reflection looked up from the pool. "Soon, you must return to Muspellheim," she said. "Tell me, bird, do you recall the volcano?"

Thundercluck thought about the fire realm and the massive, smoking mountain in the distance. He nodded.

"Within that volcano," Urd said, "Gorman Bones has carved his lair. He calls it Castle Igneous. Inside there lies a kitchen . . . the Kitchen of Destiny. That is where you will find the chef."

Thundercluck strapped on his backpack and thought, *Time to go.*

"Halt," Urd said, and the chicken paused. "Into the realms, I cannot follow," she said, "but I *can* give you relics for the battle ahead."

Thundercluck looked back at the well, where the hilt of a sword was rising to the surface.

"For Brunhilde," Urd said. The sword rose from the well and hovered in the air. It floated above the water, shimmering in the starlight from the sky. "This is a Dwarven Blade, perhaps the last in existence."

Thundercluck gazed as the blade rose higher. Then it drifted over to his backpack and snapped itself into place beside the shield. The chicken's spirits lifted.

"With that blade," Urd said, "Brunhilde will be mightier than ever before. However, the sword cannot defeat the chef. No weapon can."

The chicken's spirits dropped again.

"No weapon, no thunder, no strength of arms can vanquish Gorman Bones," Urd said. Then she whispered, "But perhaps this can."

Something else rose through the water in the well.

In the rippling pool, Thundercluck saw a pale, blurry shape. *What's that,* he wondered, *a stone? A pearl? A crystal?* It broke the surface and hovered before the chicken. It was a bar of soap.

"This," Urd said, "is the Soap of Hope. The chef has gained power with cooking spells. Every time he brews a curse"—she paused, and when she continued, her voice was grim—"he leaves a dirty dish."

Thundercluck's eyes widened.

Urd continued, "For any spell to be broken, its dish must be cleaned. Remember well the magic pie, the crusty bane of Asgard. Gorman Bones made that pie, and he cooked it in—"

The frying pan! thought Thundercluck.

"—the frying pan," said Urd. "Yes, he found a diabolical recipe . . . for

pan-fried pie. No one in Asgard could resist it." Then she smiled at Thundercluck and added, "Well, almost no one."

Thundercluck thought of Brunhilde. He caught the soap with his foot.

"For the dish to be cleansed," Urd said, "it must be scrubbed, then submerged in water with the Soap of Hope. I warn you, though: Gorman Bones will not want his kitchen trifled with, and he'll not easily part with his pan."

Thundercluck tossed the bar into his backpack.

"One more admonition," Urd said. "Once the chef has his pan at full heat, you must not let it touch you. If it does, the contact means instant death."

Thundercluck blinked. *Even so*, he thought, *I won't abandon my friend.* He stood tall and said, "Ba-gaw."

The chicken and the teller looked to the sky. Two remaining stars of Asgard still shone, but one began to flicker.

"Here the sun and moon do not shine," Urd said, "but time passes just the same."

The twinkling star faded from the sky. Only one remained.

Thundercluck looked back into the well.

Urd closed her eyes. "You have the spirit of a hero," she said. "But your enemy is treacherous indeed. You will need all your wits, all your courage, for even the slightest chance at victory. Are you ready to embark?"

When she opened her eyes, the bird was already gone.

CHAPTER 18

CHARGING THE CASTLE

THE CHICKEN RETURNED TO MUSPELL-
heim.

On his back were a sword and a shield.

In his bag was a bar of soap.

In his heart . . . there was thunder.

One last time, he looked at the stone that could send
him back to the farm. Then he turned toward the volcano. With a mighty flap of his wings, the chicken
took flight.

As Thundercluck soared, a squad of man-pigs saw him. He recalled Brunhilde's warning not to fly. The pigs fired crossbows and catapults, but Thundercluck was ready.

He blew away the arrows with a flap of his wings, then rained thunder upon the swine. The catapults crumbled, and the man-pigs fled.

Thundercluck flew on.

He soared over mountaintops until he reached the volcano. On any previous day, the flight would have exhausted him, but now he felt unstoppable.

He landed beside the volcano's lava moat, and two lava goblins rose to its surface. The creatures had rocky skin, fiery eyes,

and big, floppy ears.
They floated waist-
deep in the lava.

"There, see!" said
the bigger goblin, his
voice high-pitched and nasal. "It's that chicken, see,
the one Boss is lookin' for! I bet there's a prize if we
bring him in, see—dead or alive!"

"Yeah, yeah!" said the smaller one. They scooped
lava from the moat and hurled it at the bird.

You villains, thought Thundercluck, *just picked a fight
with the wrong chicken.*

With one wing, he blew a gust of wind that instantly
hardened the tossed lava into rocks. One thudded to
the ground by his feet, and the other bounced off his
backpack. The chicken glared at the goblins, and then,
with his other wing, he blasted a lightning bolt.

The goblins screamed and dodged as the lightning
crackled between them.

"Boss didn't say nothin' about thunder!" the smaller
goblin shouted.

"Nah, see!" yelled the bigger one. "Let's scram!"

They vanished into the lava.

I'm on a roll, Thundercluck thought. He looked over the moat and spotted a drawbridge. It was raised high, so the bird knew he would have to fly.

He paused and remembered Urd's warning: if he touched the pan at full heat, it meant instant death. He took a deep breath and thought, *At least I'll have the element of surprise . . .*

Suddenly the drawbridge lowered. The rattly gates opened wide, as if inviting him in.

Thundercluck gulped. He stepped onto the bridge.

"Buk-buk-bagock," he whispered.

Time to be brave.

Buk-buk-bagock, he thought again. *Buk-buk-bagock, indeed.*

The chicken walked into the castle, and the gates slammed shut behind him.

All was dark. Then torches burst into flame. Thundercluck gawked at the hallway's chicken art.

From up ahead, the chef's voice called, "This way, little birrrrrrd..."

Thundercluck followed the voice until he came to a grand room full of man-pigs. They stared at him from tables laden with grimy bowls. Their axes were sharp. Their faces were hungry.

"Welcome, bird," declared the chef, "to Castle Igneous!" He glared at Thundercluck from a balcony far across the room. War-Tog stood by his side. "And welcome," the Cook went on, "to my Dining Hall of Doom."

Like before, Thundercluck felt ice in his chest, but he thought, *This time I'm not going to freeze.* He waddled into the room, spread his wings, and puffed his tail feathers. *This time I'm going to fight.*

"Well, pigs," cackled the Cook, "it must be dinnertime! Let's see what's on the menu."

He held up a menu that had only I'LL HAVE THE CHICKEN written on it multiple times.

Thundercluck eyed the menu. He remembered practices with Thor and struggling to hit targets from afar. This menu was even farther away. The chicken narrowed his eyes.

ZAP!

He shot a bolt across the room. It hit the menu, frying it to ash in Gorman's hands.

"Seize him!" cried the Cook.

The man-pigs jumped to their feet. Thundercluck
held his stance and thought, *I can beat them, but I don't
have much time, and this will take a while if I'm alone!*

Ba-BAM!

A side door burst from its hinges, and Brunhilde
stood in its wake. She held an iron bar over her head
and called, "Someone check on that cage—I think it's
broken."

"What?" roared the Cook. "Who let
that girl out of her room?"

Next to the chef, War-Tog remembered giving her the nail file. His
snout drooped, and his ears went low.
Brunhilde's bag was strapped on his
shoulder, and he tried to hide it behind
his back.

The Valkyrie flew to Thundercluck. "Fancy meeting

you here," she said with a grin. "Ready for the dinner party?"

"Ba-gurrrrk!" The chicken nodded.

"I missed you, too," she said. "And you brought my shield . . . and oh! Is that a Dwarven Blade?" She tucked the iron bar in her belt and lifted the sword from the chicken's backpack. "Why, thank you, Thundercluck! What do you say, shall we give it a whirl?"

The heroes hopped into battle stances, and the man-pigs all stepped back. Then Brunhilde looked at Thundercluck, and her visor flipped open.

For just a moment, all the sass vanished from her face. Thundercluck saw softness in her eyes. A lifetime of memories rushed into his mind. "Glad you're back, buddy," she said.

Then her visor flipped back into battle mode.

From his balcony, the chef wailed, "What are you waiting for, pigs? Get them!"

"For Asgard!" cried the warrior girl.

"Ba-GWAAHHK!" cried the bird.

The pigs attacked, and the heroes fought back with

waves of magic. Brunhilde swung her Dwarven
Blade, and Thundercluck surged with power. They were
a team again, and their combined might was greater than
ever.

Kra-KOWWW!

WHOOSH!

OINK!

Man-pigs went flying in all directions. One flipped
through the air and slammed into the balcony, where
Gorman Bones grimaced. He turned to War-Tog and
yelled, "Don't just stand there! Your troops are losing;
go help them!"

War-Tog scrambled and jumped to the floor. He drew his axe and yelled, "TO GLORYYYYY—OOF!" An arc of Brunhilde's magic had hit his belly. He flew against a wall, then fell to the floor with a snort. He opened one eye at the heroes, decided not to get up, and quickly shut that eye again.

Soon all the pigs had fallen. Brunhilde bumped her fist against Thundercluck's wing, and the pair fluttered over to War-Tog.

"My pigs," he groaned. "We give up."

Brunhilde pulled the cage's bar from her belt. She

dropped it at War-Tog's feet and said, "Thanks for holding my purse."

On the balcony, Gorman muttered, "Useless swine!" He called to the heroes, "You two make a powerful pair ... Too bad you have to split!" He looked at Brunhilde. "Thor's in this castle somewhere, and you'll want to see who's with him. As for you, bird"—he fixed his gaze on the chicken—"you'll be joining me . . . in the Kitchen of Destiny!"

He backed through a door, which slammed behind him with a bang.

Thundercluck looked at Brunhilde and thought, *I'll take care of the chef.*

"If you can handle him," she said, "I'll find Thor. Deal?"

The chicken nodded and flew to the balcony. The door had an iron knob shaped like a chicken's drumstick. Once more, Thundercluck's chest went cold, but he pressed on. His foot grasped the doorknob and turned.

CHAPTER 19
COOKING UP A STORM

BRUNHILDE RETRIEVED HER BATTLE BAG
from War-Tog. The man-pig groaned again, but she
paid him no mind. She wondered, *Where is Thor?*

A few other man-pigs wheezed, but mostly the room
was quiet. Then Brunhilde heard it: a low, rumbling
snore.

I know that snore, she thought, *and it's Thor! And he's
through that door! The one on the floor!* She remembered
the tour War-Tog had given her when she first arrived.
Thor's prison was the Pantry of Peril.

Brunhilde tiptoed into the pantry. She had expected

something closet-sized, but the room was enormous and dark. A few scattered candles lit the shelves, which were lined with grim ingredients: lizard tails, fish eyes, spinach, and more. Brunhilde shivered. Then she saw Thor.

The Thunder God, still fast asleep, was chained to the far wall. Candles flickered at his feet, lighting his form against the shadows. His snores echoed in the air.

Brunhilde started toward him, but then she paused and sniffed. "Someone's breath smells familiar," she said to herself, "and it's not just Thor's."

A massive armored boar crept out from behind a shelf, moving between Brunhilde and Thor.

"Big Borris," Brunhilde muttered. "Long time, no see."

The boar snorted and stomped his hoof. The Cook had assigned him to guard Thor, and he took his job seriously. Brunhilde twirled her new blade, which glowed bright enough to light the whole pantry.

"You got the best of me last time," Brunhilde said, "but this time's different! Let's see how your fancy armor likes a Dwarven Blade!" She swung her sword and blasted an arc. The light flew at the boar, then bounced off his armor, leaving not a scratch.

"Welp," she said, "guess that answers that."

The boar charged. Brunhilde dodged sideways, sending Borris crashing by. His hooves clattered as he tried to slow down. Brunhilde sprinted over to Thor.

She broke his chains with her sword, and the sleeping god tumbled forward. Brunhilde caught him with her shield arm and let her sword go dark.

"If you were awake," she whispered to him, "your thunder could scare off the boar. Or if Thundercluck were here, *he* could scare off the boar! But I'm the only one without thunder...so how do I beat Big Borris?"

Thundercluck entered the Kitchen of Destiny. From the balcony, a winding staircase led downward to the kitchen floor. The room teemed with cabinets and countertops, all covered in dirty dishes.

At the kitchen's center, Gorman Bones stood by his cauldron. His skull and cook's hat were lit by the lava below. The chef saw the bird, and his mustache curled in a smile.

"How nice of you to join me," said the Cook. "Now, please, come closer to my cauldron."

Thundercluck wanted to keep his distance, but he remembered his goal. *Scrub the dish, then put it in water with the soap,* he thought. He narrowed his eyes at the cauldron's bubbling water. *Maybe I can get the soap in there.*

He fluttered down the staircase, and the chef said,

"Good ... Now, time to burn, chicken!"

Gorman swung his pan, shooting fire at the bird. Thundercluck jumped to evade it. In midair, he struck back with a bolt. Gorman blocked it with his pan, which erupted again with lightning and flame. The chicken landed on a dish. The Cook remained by the cauldron. They stared each other down.

Gorman grinned. "I can never seem to have a dinner party without a fight."

Thundercluck felt his pulse racing in his neck. *I can't panic,* he told himself, *and I've got to get to that cauldron!*

CRASH!

Back in the pantry, Brunhilde spun around to see what Borris had broken. In all his clambering, the beast had knocked over a jar labeled GRYPHON GREASE, and now the slimy liquid was all over his hooves.

There's an idea, Brunhilde thought. *Let's throw it against the wall and see what sticks.*

Still holding Thor with one arm, she blew out the candles on the floor. The room went mostly dark. Brunhilde lit her sword, waved it high, and called, "Over here, Borris!"

The boar charged again, and Brunhilde quickly shut off her blade, sending the room into darkness. Borris tried to slow down, but his hooves were too greasy.

He crashed against the wall, and the room shook from the impact. Various jars fell from the shelves. Borris stood up, shaken, slippery, and looking for Brunhilde.

She crouched by a shelf and grunted, propping Thor up with her shoulder. She scanned the room.

By the light of a distant candle, she noticed that one pantry wall was different from the others. The other walls were natural volcanic rock, but this one was handmade. *Hmm*, Brunhilde thought, *let's see what happens if Borris hits that!*

Thor was too heavy to carry in flight, so Brunhilde stayed low, creeping in the pantry's shadows and dragging Thor along. Borris looked around, his hooves sliding beneath him like roller skates.

Once Brunhilde was near the wall, she lit her sword again. "Hey, Borris," she called, "I'm over here!"

Again the beast charged, this time even faster, and he crashed through shelves in his way. Brunhilde leapt into the air, grunting as she pulled Thor up with her, and landed on top of the beast. Grabbing onto the boar's armor to steady herself, she ducked with Thor behind her shield.

Once more, Borris tried to stop, but once more, his feet were too greasy. With incredible speed, the girl, the god, and the boar all thundered toward the wall.

Thundercluck darted toward the cauldron. Gorman's eyes widened. He swung his pan in an uppercut, and a pillar of flame shot out of it. Thundercluck flapped his wings at the blaze, but the wind had no effect. The chicken twisted sideways, and his tail feathers caught fire.

Thwap thwap thwap!

Thundercluck beat his tail on the floor until the flames went out. He wanted to strike back at the chef, but thought, *No, my thunder's not helping . . . and my goal is that cauldron!*

The chef rained fire, and the chicken kept dodging. He made his way closer to the cauldron, but with all the sidestepping, his progress was slow.

Gorman lifted his pan high, and it began to glow red. "Behold my power," he bellowed, "when I turn up the heat!"

Thundercluck thought, *I can't let him touch me. But he's looking at the pan, not at me . . . so this is my chance!*

WHOOSH!

He flew past the Cook and landed on the cauldron's rim. Gorman spun around. He gave a toothy grin, and said, "You're making this too easy!"

The pan swung down, and this time the bird had no chance to dodge. His only defense was to push it back with a bolt.

Ba-ZAAooOOWWWW!

Streams of lightning flowed from Thundercluck's wings, and the Cook pressed into the bolt with his pan. For a moment they were locked in a stalemate. The room shook, but the Under-Cook smiled.

He pushed harder, and the pan came closer to Thundercluck. The chicken leaned away, letting his backpack dangle over the cauldron.

Through gritted teeth, the Cook snarled, "As soon as my pan touches you, bird, you're *well-done* . . . and sweet vengeance will be mine!"

Thundercluck leaned back farther, and his lightning kept flowing . . . but the pan was close! The chicken looked over his shoulder. The boiling-hot water bubbled beneath him. With his beak, he nudged his backpack open.

He felt the fiery heat coming closer. He turned back to the chef. The pan was only inches away!

Gorman Bones cackled and roared, "This is what happens when the gods play chicken . . . AND THE CHICKEN PLAYS GOD!"

Thundercluck felt a shift in his bag, and he heard a splash. *I hope that was the soap,* he thought, *'cause it's time to go!*

Just before the pan could touch him, the chicken leapt into a barrel roll and dashed to a cabinet. His breath came in heaving gulps. *After that,* he thought, *I might only have one bolt left!*

Gorman whirled and brandished his pan. He stared at the bird and screamed, "I'm not done with you yet!"

Thundercluck stepped back and felt something against his foot. He looked down and saw a scrub brush. It looked like it had never been used.

Urd's words came back to him. *Gorman Bones will not want his kitchen trifled with,* she had said. *And he'll not easily part with his pan.*

All right, thought Thundercluck, *I've got to keep my cool, and I've got to make him lose his.* The chicken grabbed the brush with his foot. *Let's get cleaning!*

"What are you doing?" snapped the chef.

Nearby, the chicken saw a dirty teacup. He hopped to it on one leg, still holding the brush with his other foot. He scrubbed some grime off the cup, and he poked the brush through its handle.

He gave the chef a calm look . . . then tossed the cup in the cauldron.

Splash!

"Stop that!" ordered the chef. "You leave my stuff alone!"

Thundercluck hopped to a metal pot, then a spatula, then a platter, scrubbing each one and adding it to the cauldron. Gorman Bones was so incredulous that for a moment he forgot to fight.

"Stop cleaning!" he shouted. "I like things how they are! I have a system! I WAS JUST LETTING THAT SOAK!"

Fury burned in Gorman's eyes, and he started thrashing with his pan. Flames roared at Thundercluck. One came so close it hit his backpack. Thundercluck caught one last glimpse of the tag—TRAGIC JACK'S MAGIC PACKS: I'VE GOT BAGGAGE!—before the whole bag was burned to ash.

He kept on dodging and scrubbing, and throwing dishes into the cauldron. Soon the big pot was overflowing, and water droplets hissed as they fell around it.

Then Thundercluck found a coffee mug with words written in its grime: WORLD'S BEST COOK.

"Don't you touch that!" Gorman snapped, paus-
ing in his tracks across the room. "That's my lucky
mug!"

Thundercluck scrubbed the grime away, and the mug's
words became faint. The Cook's bony face contorted
with rage.

The chicken hooked the mug on the brush and fluttered over to perch on the cauldron's rim. He cocked
his head at the chef.

"Don't . . . you . . . DARE drop that in there!" Gorman yelled.

Thundercluck held eye contact with the chef for a moment, then dropped the mug in the water.

Gorman howled with rage, and his pan burst into flames. Blinded by fury, the Cook threw the pan. It soared at Thundercluck like a comet on fire.

Here it comes, Thundercluck thought, and a familiar panic flashed inside him. Time seemed to slow as the frying pan came his way. Part of him had always been scared, and in his head that part was saying, *Run away! You're too weak for this!*

But the chicken answered, *No. I have one last bit of thunder, and I'm going to use it!* With his last ounce of magic, he zapped a bolt into the pan above the cauldron. The pan came to a stop, and for a moment it hung in the air. It sizzled with magic from the bolt.

Thundercluck stretched out his foot with the brush, its bristles barely reaching its target.

"Don't scrub that!" yelled the chef. "You'll ruin the nonstick coating!"

Scrub, scrub, scrub!

The pan fell into the cauldron with a splash. The water stopped bubbling, and all was quiet.

The chef looked at the bird and whispered, "What have you done?"

For a moment, nothing happened. *Uh-oh*, thought Thundercluck, and he remembered that his backpack was gone. *I managed the scrubbing and the water . . . but what if the soap wasn't in there?*

Then a single bubble rose from the cauldron and popped. Thundercluck cocked his head at the water.

BOOOOOOOOM! Bubble-bubble-bubble!

The cauldron erupted with a pillar of suds, and thunderbolts arced within it.

"Noooooooooo!" Gorman wailed. "My frying paaaaaaaaan!"

Then the floor shook, and one of the kitchen walls burst into rubble. Big Borris the Wall Buster crashed into the room with Brunhilde riding on his back. She held on to Thor, still snoring, and they tumbled to the floor.

"Oops," said the girl.

"Bagock!" said the bird.

"My kitchen!" wailed the Cook. "You don't know what you've done! I spent ages hollowing this out... That wall was holding the volcano together!"

Big Borris scrambled to his feet, his hooves still slick with grease. Thunder continued rumbling from the cauldron, and the boar panicked. He scuttled around on his hooves, then gained traction and crashed through another wall.

"Well," said Brunhilde. "I see why they call him the Wall Bus—"

BOOOOOM!

The broken walls caved in, and volcanic rocks fell from above. The castle began to collapse.

"CURSE YOU, THUNDERCLUCK!" Gorman Bones screamed, and he vanished in a puff of smoke.

Thundercluck ran to Brunhilde, who said, "Thor's still asleep, and I need your help to carry him!"

The entire volcano was shaking now, and the lava rift opened wide. The cauldron tumbled down and sank into the glow of the lava. More rocks fell, and light poured in from the volcano's top.

Brunhilde looked up and shouted, "That's our way out, but I can't carry Thor alone!"

Thundercluck nodded and said, "Ba-burrk!"

They both grabbed Thor and took flight together. They soared and spun around tumbling rocks.

The heroes emerged from the volcano and flew to a nearby cliff, where they set Thor down and watched the man-pigs running away below. The volcano trembled one last time, then imploded. When the dust settled, all that remained was a pile of rocks.

A cloud of smoke drifted upward, and the voice of Gorman Bones called out, "I'll get you next time, Thundercluck!"

Then it blew away in the wind.

Thor's eyes fluttered open. "What..." He yawned. "What happened?"

"We stopped the Cook," Brunhilde said. "Thundercluck was so brave—you should have seen him!"

The chicken swelled with pride.

Brunhilde pointed at the rocks and said, "Gorman's gone. Thundercluck cleaned his kitchen."

CHAPTER 20
OVER AND DONE

OVER THE FOLLOWING WEEK, THUNDER-
cluck, Brunhilde, and Thor made their way back to Asgard. The trip home was smoother than the journey
out had been. This time the heroes knew the path, and
they walked with newfound confidence. The bird had
his power back, the girl had her new blade, and Thor
was with them all the way.

Asgard had risen from its sleep, and the realm was
grateful to its champions. When the travelers arrived,
Valhalla's army lifted Thundercluck and Brunhilde
on their shoulders, and the Vikings carried the pair
through all the kingdom.

Hennda swelled with pride in her son. Saga finally wiped the pie off her face, and she gave Brunhilde a nod. Even the lion statue, still clutching the yarn from Brunhilde's graduation day, seemed to smile.

Back on the farm, Olga and Sven woke early to a knock on the door. There was no one on their doorstep, but a figure with a gray beard stood in the field.

"Odin?" Sven called, but the figure vanished in a beam of rainbow light.

"What's this?" Olga asked, and she pointed at their feet. There was a bouquet of flowers and a scroll.

They unraveled the scroll, which read:

HE SAVED US. WITH A VALKYRIE'S GUIDANCE, THUNDER-CLUCK SAVED US ALL.

They heard a gentle squeak and looked up. On their roof was a new weather vane, crafted from Asgardian gold. It was chicken-shaped like their last one, but while the old vane had seemed bored, this one looked ready for adventure. It sparkled in the new dawn.

On the back of the scroll, they also saw:

THANK YOU FROM ALL THE REALMS.

—THOR & ODIN

NICE MEETING YOU! —BRUNHILDE

BAGOCK. —THUNDERCLUCK

With Asgard's glory restored, Thundercluck and Brunhilde surveyed the kingdom. Saga and Thor joined them atop Mount Fjell. The sun was setting in the west, and a thunderstorm rumbled in the east. Above the clouds, nine stars twinkled in the sky.

Thundercluck was the first to take flight, giving a triumphant "Ba-GOCK!" as he soared.

Brunhilde lingered behind, and Thor put his hand on her shoulder.

"You should join him," Thor said. "You were there in his time of need; now, you can share his joy. You've made us all proud."

Brunhilde smiled at Thor. She was almost ready to fly, but first she gave Saga a hug. Then she took off, leaving the Gods of Thunder and Vision together on the mountain.

Saga smiled as the friends flew by.

"Is it over?" asked Thor. "Is Gorman Bones forever gone?" Saga turned to the west. She squinted into the sunset. After a pause, she looked to the heroes and said:

Perhaps the Cook will strike again;
his fate remains unknown.

But with the Battle Maiden's help,
our feathered friend has grown.
When monsters come! When danger knocks!
When evil runs amok!
We have ourselves a chicken now.
We have our Thundercluck!

EPILOGUE

FROM THE VALLEY OF DAL, KING ODIN AND
Queen Frigg watched the heroes flying above.

"You're sure, then?" Frigg asked.

"Yes," Odin answered. "Saga confirms, and thus it is true." The elder god stared at the sky. "We were lucky Thundercluck saw the Well of Eternity alone. Had Brunhilde been with him, she might have learned the truth."

"So..." said Frigg, gazing at the Valkyrie. "Brunhilde still doesn't know about her parents."

"No." Odin sighed. "Not yet. But as Saga has foretold, she *will* learn. Now the girl wields the Dwarven Blade. Someday she will meet the one who held it first."

Frigg nodded and said, "We can only hope she'll be ready."

PAUL TILLERY IV lives in Raleigh, North Carolina. He's always loved drawing, storytelling, and off-kilter comedy. He earned his MFA in animation from SCAD Atlanta in 2014 and taught animation at SCAD in Savannah, Georgia. *Thundercluck!* is his first book. thundercluck.com

Co-illustrator **MEG WITTWER** was born in Fort Wayne, Indiana. She enjoys drawing and communicating with others through art and collaboration. She also digs birds (especially chickens). Meg earned her BFA in illustration from SCAD in 2016 and now works as an illustrator in Atlanta, Georgia. megillustration.com

ACKNOWLEDGMENTS

Paul and Meg both thank their agent, Melissa Nasson of Rubin Pfeffer Content, and their team at Roaring Brook Press, particularly Connie Hsu, Megan Abbate, and Christina Dacanay.

FROM PAUL

Thundercluck! began as an animated short film; Paul thanks James Hunt, Dandy Barrett, and Brandon Bush for their crucial roles in the film's production.

For feedback on early drafts of the book, Paul thanks Phil Bailey, Meaghan Walsh Gerard, Stacy Carter, Christopher Soucy, Jeremiah Kizer, and Mary Doll. Paul also thanks his family for their encouragement, and David Sterritt for his endless moral support.

Meg was the first person to read the book's full first draft, and Paul remains deeply thankful she agreed to join the project.

FROM MEG

Meg would like to thank Paul, who trusted her enough to let her join him on *Thundercluck!* Life would've been worlds different without Brunhilde and Thundercluck.

For their never-ending support and trust, Meg gives her thanks and love to her wonderful parents, Elissa and Anthony. And for his words of encouragement, Meg thanks her brother Aaron.

HOLD ON TO YOUR FEATHERS!

THE SECOND BOOK IN THE THUNDERCLUCK!
SERIES WILL BE AVAILABLE

FALL 2019